AUTHOR'S NOTE

This book was written in 2000. We were living in Belgium then and the light was so pure that I knew how The Lowlands had formed her great painters.

I'd been researching a long novel for a year or so but had come to a standstill. What was my story exactly? I thought that the book had beaten me and I called myself a stupid man and cursed the book and cursed my wasted time. I slung the stalled book in a drawer.

But the news from England was of the e-commerce boom. The new economy was rouletting bogus fortunes into young and willing laps. I was reading and re-reading the immaculate *Great Gatsby*, and that book, the heartbreaking, beautiful dusks, and those sluicing, gorgeous fortunes must have clung together in my mind. About a week after I banished the long novel, I found *Light*.

CRAIG TAYLOR

LIGHT

reverb

reverb is an imprint of Osiris Press Ltd

This edition first published 2005 by

Osiris Press Ltd
PO Box 615
Oxford OX1 9AL

www.readreverb.com
www.osirispress.co.uk

A CIP catalogue record for this book is available from the British Library

ISBN 1 905315 00 7

Set in Baskerville 12/14.2pt
Title font Acerina (www.hulahula.com.mx)

Printed in Britain by
Lightning Source, Milton Keynes

Published in association with Shed Books

for Anna

east

I

Until the morning he arrived at my father's funeral in a wine-stained, white linen suit, I had not seen Will for ten years. It was speculated in the chapel that he was a loan shark from the period of gambling which preceded my father's death. In truth, my friendship with Will spanned much of my childhood; though as he is two years older, it naturally faltered between our staggered puberties, and in the four years before he left for college we were not close. For a long time I venerated our prior closeness: days of arson by his lake, dens and feasting in his elaborate house.

Hours after the funeral he drove me to the station. I had work the next day and needed to catch the last train to London. He stood with me on the platform and I looked at him and liked him. Apparently he was speaking:

"... When my son was born, my parents gave us the house and moved to France."

"Tell me about the suit Will."

He smiled suddenly, then as suddenly again was serious.

"On the day I left the village, your father came to see me. He had a white linen suit which he said no longer fitted him. He said it was perfect for weddings and summer and he made me promise to wear it. The first time I wore it was ten years ago. I drenched it with wine and ruined it. The second time was today."

The train clanged lazily into the station and I shook Will's hand. Through the window, I looked upwards to name and savour the stars before London took them.

❧

My father had a long and slender nose, along which his brown-rimmed glasses would travel as he observed a war documentary, a bird's flight or an argument. He had a pale, blank face and a shining oblong forehead draped with weak, capricious hair. He was weak, I think, and surprised by life and his voice had raised eyebrows in it. There was something of the consumptive about him, some waxy yellow under his thin and shining skin. And something of the saint also, though I concede that the keenness of bereavement naturally sanctifies the dead.

There is a wedding photo buckled with handling. It shows the plump face of my mother and the smooth face of my father. Relatives stand around them, flowers pinned to the slim lapels of chain-store suits – rarely-worn clothes beautifying grim and battling faces. Mother is proud in the photo, her chin is held slightly upwards as she looks into the camera. She is relieved no doubt to escape the teeming house of the many sisters and the patched and re-patched skirts. And she is proud perhaps of her husband; her hard-working, taciturn and kind new husband.

Father is glancing to the left. If you follow his eyes he is looking at the vicar, who proselytises the camera with a wide grin of Anglican teeth. A remote smile lays on his face, his lips are thin and tightly pursed. It is the smile of a dream, perhaps. And even then there is the crumpled circle tensed in his brow, about the size of the tie knot snuggled below his chin. The brow holds some vexation, some anticipation of future events. The puzzle of moving time hangs around him.

If death comes to all, can it be tragic, can it be anything but banal? I don't know. A verdict of accidental death was recorded, so said the local paper. Did they get it right? Partially. Accidental life may have been more accurate. I think he was a beautiful man, and if he were not for this earth, it remains difficult to imagine another on which he would have thrived.

When he was made redundant he would rise at seven, shave carefully across his eczema and slip a clean shirt over his shoulders. Then he would stand in the lounge and drink tea, glancing across his watch. In these first months, she said, he looked like he was listening, waiting for a signal – the blurt of a horn outside or the phone awakened by his boss's volte-face. With my father at home, the small garden was treated, it grew impeccably clipped.

He climbed from bed and sleep-walked through the dark hallway of the bungalow. He was standing in front of the phone table, lifting the car keys off the wooden hook, when she found him. She turned him and eased him towards the bedroom. He awoke and she made him coffee, and sat through his tears and crumpled owlish blinking.

He invested his redundancy pay-off with a former colleague. They planned to renovate a barn in the next village and sell it to an interloper. The friend went to Spain with the money and took his cousin's wife. The lawn remained trimmed, the reddening skin shaved.

He visited the Jobcentre for help with his retraining. He was going to be a gardener. They said he was too old, "Too old to dig," he said, "Too old for fucking flowers."

My mother told me that. It was the first time she'd heard him swear. He got part-time work at home, soldering components into circuit boards. It was not enough – the money was dripping out of the house and the drink was growing inside him. On the day of his funeral I found an empty vodka bottle hidden in the garden.

He lost £800 on the Epsom Derby the first time he stepped inside a bookmaker's. It came on that quickly. She sobbed in the worn brown chair and the light frittered through the curtains. The bookies owed him money, so he thought, and he gave them more to get it back. Arguments filled the house. Old hurts recovered by new swirled around the dark sideboard and the deep brown box of the television. Separate bedrooms were adopted, my father's twitching sleep observed by the posters of my former heroes. And my mother weeping in the mirror and combing her hair with the thick black brush she was given by her mother. The brush had wild flowers enamelled on its back and lay on a dulled silver plate. She didn't care about the ring, she only wished he'd asked.

I don't suppose they called themselves loan sharks when he met them in the pub. They were just two men who would lend him the money to get his back. He was absent from the house now as much as he was able. But he had nowhere to go and stayed in bed, listening to the radio under itchy white blankets. Mother's sisters began to visit more often. He stopped leaving the racing papers in the lounge and folded them up and pushed them in a clump under the bed.

My mother didn't want him to move out – she didn't want him to stay either – but he said he had to. It was the shame, he said – easier to take when alone. Shame gangs up with other people, amplifies itself through your love for them. She would drive over to see him in the bedsit, taking meals for him to freeze in his jammed-up ice box. She missed him. Some habitual pride kept her moving through the world.

My father's landlord stopped coming to collect the rent. Perhaps he couldn't bear to see him, perhaps he forgot. I doubt he forgot. I went to see my father once. I sat down in a sticky vinyl chair. The old kettle whistled as he smiled at me. The smile was like the wedding day smile. "I told you," it almost said. He showed me a picture of his new friend. She had long dry hair. They were sat together in the pub. He looked hearty under her drunken kiss. It cost me a lot, but I said I was glad. I gave him twenty quid and some fruit. He said he'd come and see my new flat in London. We both knew he wouldn't.

The local paper informs us when they called, fins showing. My penniless father hid from them out on the window ledge. He tumbled onto the concrete. It was late afternoon and his body attracted the school children. Fall? Jump? Irrelevant. The body made it irrelevant.

After the funeral, my mother went to stay with her sisters in the States. She tried to have a holiday. She called me once from Disneyland. What was she doing? Living I suppose. Living now with death – laughing with her sisters in Disneyland, California, above the San Andreas fault.

My parents married when they were twenty. When they were my age I was seven. We no longer must wed the first we bed. We have choice. At twenty – at thirty even – we are wedded to the self: education, career, travel, promiscuity. We are bound to the imperative of choice – consuming, democratised individuals demand self-betterment. What can we really choose? Little, I say. But then I believe in chance, not choice: chance and accident. And I think that we are stooges and beauties and children and monkeys: our mistakes really choose for us, and our families, and our wallets, and our love. And character – inexplicable, accidental character – chooses also.

I think I can tell when it's going to rain. I feel the air changing in my chest. Don't cows sit down before it comes? It will rain soon. The wet will fall on trees and roads. Brakes will slowly skid. Accidents will happen.

❧

At nineteen, with no navigable direction, I mooched around my parents' house. I ate breakfast cereal and wore the karate pyjamas I had been bought for my thirteenth birthday. I still have them. I conceived a vague and great notion to travel, worked in local bars, got free rent and board from my folks, and within a year had passport, injections and £8,000.

In India I fell in love. We met at the Taj Mahal. She was an Australian, travelling for a single week before returning to the leper's school which she ran on the plains of Uttar Pradesh. I was braving a two-week skirmish with the dusty subcontinent before returning to my reptilian languor among the beach bars of Thailand. She spent two nights at my hotel. We ate well and laughed. Three years later she left me and I left India with a clearer idea how to teach lepers. Quite why I then followed her back to Australia when she had made it viciously clear that our relations were over, I cannot say. Nor can I explain the three years I spent working on a fruit farm in Queensland. I do not understand these six years of lepers and mangoes – I have only these words: "I loved her."

I met Donald at the fruit farm – another peripatetic labourer. We laughed at each other's jokes as we ricked our spines picking in the field. Is it fair to say that Donald is the only person who has ever made me happy? So far, yes.

Donald taught me how to paint, and he said I was good at it. "You're good," he said. We would come in from the fruit fields after work and go to the barn where the farm owner let Donald keep a studio. We'd open a couple of bottles of cheap wine and get stoned and go at the painting; really go at it, like a couple of household decorators reacquainted with their childhood epilepsy. We couldn't often afford canvas so we used what we could find. My best painting was done on an old, discarded white wooden door. It was a speculative piece called *My Wife's House*. Maybe it's still in the barn.

I was sad when we went our separate ways. Donald gave me one of his paintings and took a plane. I came home then.

The first few months back were bad. I was broke. Most of my friends had moved away, while those who'd stayed were kind but unavailable – ensconced in pervasive domesticity. I stayed with my parents and felt the imminence of their divorce. I visited the Jobcentre and was offered work in a mushroom factory or an abattoir. I was twenty six and felt like a teenager. Enough.

I needed cash and I needed out, needed friends also. I massaged my CV to demonstrate a career trajectory, borrowed from my mother to buy a suit, and kept my nerve through a job interview with a media sales company in central London. I worked there for a year, embracing the wage labour, sexual tension and alcoholism that comprise the public face of the capital. I had friends and money and my life began to assume some of the repetitive solidity it had in childhood. I even had sex. I was a grown up. I thought I was going to make it.

Then, as you know, my father died. Seven days after the funeral my mother commenced her long visit to her sisters. Twenty eight days after that I was 'let go'. We all were. *Contemporary Aviation* and its sister title, *Yesterday's Aviation*, went under. They were our main clients. All the ex-staff went out drinking in Soho. We complimented each other and confessed who we'd fancied. There was laughter and we felt better. I went home and looked at my painting.

It's like this:

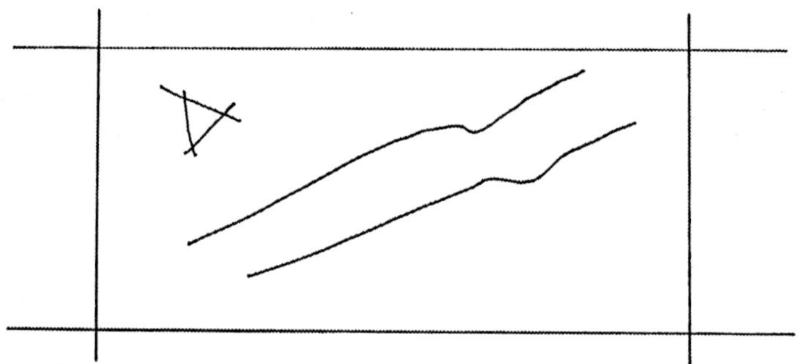

It's better, though. Like all Donald's work, it's abstract. Donald lives in America now. You can email him on donald_birkin30@thoughtplay.com. I shouldn't give you his address, but he's a nice guy. He'd take it as a chance to make friends. Donald likes old films and he likes to sleep outside. He has a GSOH; smokes fags though.

For two unattractive weeks I was drunk. I was bereaved and clueless and single and poor. I recited mantras of my own inadequacies and grew hostile towards things which reminded me of me. Late at night in loud expensive bars I felt lecherous then bitter, hating my stringy legs and simian head – oh wretched, ugly urban man. Was I falling apart? Was the good ship sinking? It seemed that way.

Then Will called me.

"...Ben, I know you'll be finding things hard, and, because, well I've got an offer... Our gardener-handyman-type person has just died too, and, and I thought well... There's a nice room for you here and you'll get money. Enough to go to the pub and things... I know you're not qualified or anything but you'll be fine. And I'm at home. I mean I'm at home all the time now and it would be fun..."

Beam me up!

Will pulled up outside my flat two days later. I crammed some bags into his archaic sports car and we drove East – *tally ho!* It was seven years since I had lived in the village. Now for one long summer I would live there again.

II

The driveway unfolded in a lazy ache and I looked up to the house, its wide face rubbed to orange by the late sun. On the far side of the house, ramshackle outbuildings sloped around a pebbled courtyard. Horses strolled in a large rolling field and above the sky was huge. We pulled into the courtyard and climbed out of the car.

Will bounded up the steps, standing half inside the open doorway.

"Archie! Jessica!"

He turned and looked at me. He was unshaven and he played with his hands. I was flattered by his nervousness, by the importance of my entrance. I was also surprised. Aged twelve I had read First World War books, some by survivors of the Western Front. When new soldiers arrived, the veterans could tell who would live and who would die in the mud. Some recruits had a glow around them, a smell of luck, and the old hands stuck close to them to share their fortune. When I read of this, I had thought of Will, sensed a glow of survival round him. I venerated him then, I was a willing duckling imprinted on his munificence, on the knack of his coincidental impunity.

And I am still not free of the dazzle of Will; still not over it, even now after the events of that long, wet summer.

Archie arrived. I had not met this little boy before. Each step he slapped on the stone was a potential skull cracker. His father snatched him up and briefly held their faces close, "See, looks like me."

"He does." He didn't. Archie lost his face in his father's neck.

"Where's your mother, Archie?"

"'Undun," yelped the boy.

"Who's here with you?" Will asked abruptly.

"'Swarze."

He turned to me. "He means Françoise, the au pair. Come in, come in."

He beckoned me forward with his non-Archie arm and I stepped into the hallway.

Little had changed. The furniture still sedate and solid, the floor tiles still cracked and geometric. Old feelings rose. I had always felt envious of Will's home: no, not envious – precision – it had always made me feel flimsy, like a straw man. Not the size of Will's estate, not the value, not the drip feed of cash from relatives' deaths. It wasn't Will's money that made me feel vulnerable. It was the other wealth that went through the house: the aunts and uncles who played music on the patio and sang well in the bathrooms; the people called 'auntie' and 'uncle' who came and scattered accomplishments through the rooms then drove off to concerts and openings and other friends. It was the godmothers and godfathers and the painters and actors and the linguists and waifs who came to the house. It was the twenty types of everything in the fridge and on the bar, and the cars on the drive and the people on the phone. It was the solidity of Will's life, its buoyancy, the sense that he lived in the centre of a warmly rippling lake, and all he need do was relax and paddle slowly towards the shore. There were always voices in Will's house.

We walked into the kitchen. As before, a long-legged

table lay down the centre of the room, cut from the trunk of a single hardwood tree. Jars and canisters and pots stood scattered across the marble surfaces: tea and coffee and malt drinks and fresh herbs and spices and sauces and gadgets. A thin trail of spilled pulses curled at my feet and old panelled walls gave way to the huge back larder. By the window a paint-splattered radio spoke to itself. We sat down, Will and I on chairs, grubby Archie on the floor. Will smiled at me and he opened and closed his mouth. He stood and walked over to the chromium kettle.

"Tea? Jess keeps all these rare breeds, but I'm a basics man."

"Basic's fine."

He sat down and pushed a teapot towards me. I took the top off and looked inside. It was full of weed.

"Keeps me out of mischief now I'm a bored house husband. Help yourself."

I smiled and put the top back on. Will stood again and walked over to the windowsill, picking up a picture frame and handing it to me.

"Always keep this here…"

It was a photo of my family, displaying the gaudy imperfections of 1970s colour processing. I am vain I suspect because I always look at myself first in photos. Perhaps everyone does? I shall ask. In the photo I am wearing a jacket which I can remember loving dearly. Not because of any intrinsic properties of the jacket, but because my parents didn't want to buy it for me. It was a treasure of self assertion and it was burgundy. My father looked happy. He didn't like to be photographed but here he smiled. I was cuddled under my mother's arm and her hair was pushed back with the wind. I think we were by the sea. There was some thrill of salt air in our cheeks.

The au pair came in and bobbed her eyes about then walked away. There were some magazines under her arm and three large dogs followed her. I looked at the boy on the floor.

"Why 'Archie'?"

Will's gaze rested on a tea cup, "We were down in Exeter when Jessica was pregnant. She'd never been and we wanted, well it was Remembrance Sunday and we went inside the Cathedral. There were hundreds of little palm crosses behind the altar, and I was just looking at them. They all had little messages on them. One was,

Archie Higgins 1920 – 1939
I Love You,
Vi

I just got thinking, and the woman who wrote that had been in love with a dead man for nearly sixty years. It just stayed with me. And when I was at the birth and I saw him, I just shouted 'Archie', which was a bit embarrassing. Then the nurses started calling him it, which Jess said was unprofessional. And it just worked out that way. Jessica hates it, says it's my name."

I looked over his shoulder, looked out into the garden and watched the dark begin to cluster slowly among the branches and the flowers and leaves. It seemed a beautiful story. My grandfather fought in the war. He wore a beard to hide his scars. He wasn't called Archie, though. Albert was his name. Archie's a nice name.

We fetched my boxes and bags from the car and Will showed me upstairs to his parents' old room. It was big and sported a four poster bed and a suit of armour. I calculated how much certain Americans would pay to stay there.

"Not a bad room for a handyman," Will said, plumping a pillow.

"A non-handy handyman at that."

"There's not much to do really, it'll be fine. I'll take you round the gardens before it gets too dark. Jess has devised some 'tasks'."

The descent of a wide, slowly curved staircase took us to the door, and we walked across the pebbles of the courtyard down into the long back garden. The last swifts deferred to the veering tack of bats and the lawn was sad as jade. Cuckoos repeated what cuckoos repeat. We walked down the crumbling stone steps into the vegetable garden, a tangled mass of non-linear root crops and burgeoning, fibrous stalks.

"First thing. Get the veggies into the kitchen. Our old gardener failed to do that. Don't know why really. Grew huge things and left them."

More steps took us down to the walled gardens. Trained pear trees grew geometric shoulders, and huge roses tangled up from kidney-shaped flower beds. A broken wooden bench rotted by the pond and reflected across the orange daubs of listless fish.

"Second thing, get the heating going in this garden."

As I knew from my childhood, a small shed below housed a boiler which connected to pipes running through the walls – up which tropical plants could grow through temperate air. But, as I also knew from my childhood, the boiler was cantankerous, expansive and unfathomable. Will walked towards the shed and I followed him. We stepped inside. The air was musty and dense. White spores grew on the soil floor. Mostly broken tools lay in corners and rusting cans of god-knows-what trooped wonkily along dust-grey shelves. The dull metal of the boiler loomed on the left. Will's mobile phone went off.

"Excuse me." He stepped outside.

I walked forward and picked up a spade from the corner of the shed, weighing it in my hand. Its flat, chipped face was rutted with rust. I mimed digging. After one year of computer screens – the mailing of pitches and promotional circulars; the intranet strategy groups and projected quotas – this digging, this actual doing, would seem absurd.

Will extended his head around the doorway.

"Jessica. On her way. Driving. She'll be here in an hour."

We walked from the garden, down more steps and through the avenue which led to the lake. We stood for a moment under a high pine, its branches hugging over towards the water. I looked across the lake to a colony of geese on a small island, then beyond them to the barns on the far side of the water.

"Sue lives there now," Will said, nodding at the barns.

"I thought they were derelict?"

"They were but Sue fell in love. She's having them kitted out. They're going to be amazing."

"Who's Sue?"

"You'll see. She's having a party tomorrow. You're invited. You'll probably recognise her, she's been in the papers recently. Went to college with Jess – poor Northern girl, Jess claims. Says she discovered her. Sue's done very well for herself... I'll let you into a secret. It's Jessica's thirty-first soon and Sue's organised a surprise for her. All will be revealed tonight. Come on."

Will turned and walked back up the garden, his hands in his pockets, a boyish whistle rising from his lips. I took a quick look back to the lake and the barns then followed him.

She arrived as we sat in Will's study, rolling peaty whiskey round thick and crystal glasses. It was about 10:30. I had never met Jessica before. She stood in the doorway, freeing her long hands: one yellow glove's fingertip nipped in her childishly white teeth as she disengaged the other. Her hair was cropped up against a nifty skull and she wore no make-up. She was breathless and she smiled at me. It was a burnished and slight smile, inviolable and moneyed. A smile which knew its strengths. Her lips looked sticky. She flipped her fingers forward and glanced down her nails, stepping forward to shake my hand. She may have been drunk. I stood and lunged my hand forward. The wands of her fingers flitted into my palm.

"Jessica. Pleased to meet you. Will's told me much. Much. Nothing too bad. Sit down. So, the garden and the heating and the lake will need dredging. A drink darling. Something long. White spirits. Had to pop to the flat."

She collapsed backwards into an enormous chair and

pulled her knees up under her chin, then she peered exhaustedly forward, inching off her shoes and rubbing the ball of her left foot, an ear cocked towards the window.

"No deer tonight?"

"Too early love." Will handed her a glass.

She sloshed her ice around a little, prodded her lemon and looked at me.

"We have deer barking here at night. Sometimes right through. They're very rare though and sweet. Quite small. Settled in?"

I nodded. She rolled forward and looked at me, her lips and forehead taut.

"I heard about your father. Soz... Will does love you, you know – childhood summers, shit pies, bike ramps and all that. I've heard it all. He was nervous about you coming, thought it meant more to him than you and that... and that you wouldn't know each other I suppose."

She clapped a palm down onto a chair arm and a little dust rose.

"Will's in a rough patch so be nice."

I looked at Will and felt warmth cluster in my throat and cheeks. I did not know if the warmth arose from shame or affection. Will shifted feet and stroked the crown of his hair, staring at Jessica.

"Anyway," she continued, "I'm going to fix you up with Sue. You're obviously the sort of person she'll like."

"What sort of person is that, Jessica?"

"Oh god, you know."

She stood and moved to the door, throwing some words over her shoulder.

"Got to change. See you for dinner."

I turned to Will. "Do you want to talk about it?"

"Yes but no but there's nothing to say."

As the vegetarian au pair was cooking, and as Jessica claimed intolerance to gluten, and Will insisted on bulk, we ate a meal of microwaved jacket potatoes with salad and cheese around the huge kitchen table. The cutlery chimed loudly, then grated across emptied plates. The au pair sloped off in heavy socks to watch TV in her room and Will went upstairs to check on Archie.

With a confidential movement of her wrist, Jessica poured me a glass of wine.

"We should be friends. We should talk. Will hasn't got any money left, his family are virtually paupers. He just strolls around this big house and everyone thinks he's loaded. He should be working. Not doing this bread-baking daddy thing. I think he's lost it. *Will-o'-the-wisp* I call him."

"And what do you do Jessica?"

"I do very well."

The phone rang. It was a friend of Jessica's wanting travel advice. Jessica gave her some travel advice.

Will came down and joined me at the table, then he stood and walked to the fridge, sliding a hot dog sausage from an open can and biting it in half. After many goodbyes, each increasing in proximity to the next, Jessica put down the phone.

"There's someone here to see you Jessie."

"Who? Are they nice?"

"I'll bring them in."

Will came back with a short, wide woman, her huge hair wrestled backwards by a tattered yellow band and a carefully thrust pencil. Her teeth were grey and her eyes were reddened, lively with amiable contempt. She was very cigarettes. She wore an old black sweatshirt and loose black trousers. I liked her. She moved towards Jessica, her hand held out. Jessica lowered hers.

"Hello Jessica, I'm your birthday present. I'm Maggie Twist."

"Maggie Twist?" Wondered Jessica unconvincingly.

"I'm an artist."

"Do you sell?"

"I am bought."

"She won the Constable Prize last year," aided Will.

"Oh yes, I do remember, *Wrecking Bassoons*, the video piece."

"Right. I believe you know my husband."

"Do I?" Jessica again wondered unconvincingly.

"Yes. Pavel."

"Oh yes, Pavel. So you're my present?"

"Sue's commissioned me to paint your husband, your son and herself. She wants to call it 'Three People Who Love Jessica'..."

"... What a present!"

"I'm painting over at Sue's. Part of the present is for you to watch the work. I'll be staying there until it's done."

"She paying well?"

❧

Later, I walked down to the lake and sat cross-legged on a low stone pedestal, its deposed Grecian urn wrapped in ivy at its base. The water was still. Geese absorbed the moonlight and lights blazed from the roofs of the old barns. I saw a figure on the far side of the lake. Sue maybe. A boozy female laugh jumped into the trees. I couldn't make out her face.

I sat for a while, coveting the stars then I walked back inside and stood outside the kitchen door. Evidently Maggie had departed.

"We said we wouldn't leave him alone Jess."

"Why do you think we've got the au pair? I had to go."

"The au pair's a kid."

"Why have her? You worry too much. Sacred bloody baby."

"Who did you see in town?"

"Oh god what is the point."

"You tell me. I'm just..."

"You're not even listening to me."

"I'm just..."

"You're not even listening to me."

I padded up to my room.

III

I had been working in the garden all day, discerning the difference between vegetable and weed, and listening to the cars rattle someway along the drive then break off right towards Sue's barns. I had cleaned my nails in the bathroom, smoothed my newly acquired calluses, and dressed carefully so as to look like I did not care how I looked. I wanted to make love on this sweet summer night.

The moon was high already as we walked from the house. Will remained inside, watching over Archie. Jessica's nostrils twitched as we moved through the garden. She slipped her arm through mine.

"Excited?"

I nodded. I was.

"Good. Should be. There'll be lots of faces."

We rounded the dark lake. Soft electronic music and the murmur of voices purred up from around the barns. Leaves flicked in the breeze. We breached a gap between two buildings and entered a three-sided cobbled square, the fourth side open to the trees and a wide flat field behind it. Pallets and cement and varied woods lay piled against a wall and a stage was built in front of a wide oak. Amps and guitars and electronica stood unused across it. A yellow marquee was rigged to the left of the square. People stood in groups, lolling and talking and laughing. Sea Breezes mingled with Caipirinhas on a ping-pong table wheeled out as an impromptu bar. I smelled the trees and the summer.

Jessica's arm twitched in mine.

"Hello? Are you there?"

"Yes."

"Who do you want to meet first?"

I raised my shoulders.

"Well," Jessica nodded towards a darkly-dressed group stood under red and yellow lanterns, "they're all music. And," she frowned towards a groomed and garrulous knot of people standing in front of the stage, "they're TV… And these here," she curled her hand out to the left, "these people are the new economy."

Then, her voice peppered discreetly with malice, she laughed and said, "Roll a bomb over there and the city would go bats in the morning. Let's start with them." She tugged my shirt a little and I stepped forward, my throat now dry.

"Do you want a drink?"

"Yes. Fizzy. I'll be here." She winched a finger out in the direction of the new economy.

At the ping-pong table, my impecunious fingers hovered over free drinks, restraining themselves to lift but two. Maggie Twist appeared to my left.

"You didn't say much last night."

"Don't usually."

"Who are you then, Jessica's gimp?"

"My name's Ben, I'm a friend of Will's."

"That's my husband."

She indicated a tall, dark-skinned man, his arms clasped behind his back, leaning slightly forward to listen to a small girl in a white dress. He swung slowly, coyly at his hips, and nodded with astute comprehension.

"Everybody's fucking him…"

I looked across to Jessica, engrossed by her own voice as it ricocheted into a sleekly-dressed man, his furtive nodding betraying something like panic.

"... Everybody is," confirmed Maggie, a vital laugh pranging from her throat. "Even me."

She waved a cigarette box in front of me.

"No."

"Come and meet someone."

I followed Maggie across the courtyard towards the far barn, its draughty door swinging open. Dark slender wheat waved across the field, and further lurked a black copse of bulked oak. A single room stretched out darkly, an old piano in its centre.

"There's nobody here."

"I know. Cocaine?"

I demurred and she opened a small wrap of powder on top of the piano then rolled a note and snorted.

"We're doing a performance piece here later. Will you film it for me?"

"And become a famous artist?"

"If you like."

"Sure, I'll... Is it hard? I mean do you want cuts and effects?"

"No. Just point and film."

"What's the piece about?"

"It's called *Three Against Art.* Me and two Spanish friends are going to kick this in." She patted the piano.

"Do you like art Ben?"

"I think your thing's a bit stupid."

"But you'll do it?"

"Yes, I..."

"Good, you're good. I'll give you a painting."

"I own a painting."

"Really?"

"A Donald Birkin."

"I know him. Donald and his fey abstracts. You'd have got a lot of cash for that a few months ago. But he's in remission now."

We went back into the courtyard.

A man with a mountainous nose and a thick French accent was being harangued by a well known film director. The Frenchman coughed, strapped a sarcastic smile to his face and disappeared into a clump of TV girls by the bar. The director rolled his shoulders and straightened his bootlace tie.

Will had arrived and stood slightly behind Jessica, hands in pockets, bobbing his head to suggest interest in a futuristically-dressed woman. Maggie pinched my arm and whispered, "Going to prime the Spaniards. You helping me later?"

I nodded and she collapsed her fingers into her palm, then revived them in mock, miniature salute. I returned to the bar, this time brazenly lifting several glasses, then I stood against a slender tree and drank. Quick, jabbing sounds jumped from the amps and I looked over to see four men strolling the stage, checking instruments from inside tenty anoraks. The band began to play.

A review was posted on a music site next day, and zinged to fashionable inboxes soon after.

❧

Fwd: Smash Up Your Instruments

To: jay_brockledent@thoughtplay.com

Cc:

Subject: Fwd: Smash Up Your Instruments

Account: Keeku Astor <keeku_astor@thoughtplay.com>

DONT USUALLY MAIL OUT NONSENSE IN WORK HOURS. BUT CHARLIE SENT ME THIS AND I COULDNT RESIST. VERY FUNNY.

PLANS FOR W/END?

KEEKS

Smash Up Your Instruments

Aiming to announce his rehabilitation to the opinion-forming classes, esoteric and karate-loving singer Danni Red made his first public appearance in six years on a small stage at millionaire e-cialite Sue Watson's country house in Suffolk, England tonight. Following the demise of his first band Mudfugger, and his residency at a number of expensive clinics, Red, currently without record contract, played a shambolic set of old and new songs to an initially bemused then increasingly alienated crowd of key entertainment fixers.

Beginning with a brace of leggy acoustic canters, Red's performance quickly disentangled into vague drunken incident. As prominent television executives called each other wankers in bushes, the increasingly indolent Red, sporting a canary yellow tracksuit, left the stage and fell among bottles. The lank-haired singer spent ten minutes at the bar, as his keyboard player, percussionist and loyal 'vibes-man' Brick lamely noodled across their instruments. Returning to the stage with three of his brothers, the gig took on the aspect of an embarrassing Christmas knees-up as Red coerced his siblings through a medley of Bee Gees and Beach Boys vocal harmonies.

The next two songs were breathy numbers. As the band disagreed on tempo, their rasping frontman improvised a-rhythmic vocals about "pies and fruit". Gurning Red rounded off his set with a surprisingly resolute version of 'Love Me Tender', then kicked his stool, drank wine and did crack. Vibes-man Brick left the stage and passed among the audience touting for change with a sun hat. But this was not to be the last of bad art for the night and Red's encore was still to come.

Later in the evening, Earner prize-winning artist Maggie Twist meticulously destroyed a piano, aided by silent Iberian accomplices. The act was filmed by her new collaborator, an introverted young man with a simian forehead whom she claimed would soon be recognised as "the greatest artist on earth", but who told me he was a gardener. Embittered by the attention directed at the artists, a by-then-twatted Red approached the plant-loving auteur and clubbed him effectively with maracas. Red was quickly sedated by the band and placed in his van.

While the wounded gardener was spotted dancing with hostess Sue Watson at dawn, it seems difficult to imagine a new morning for self-stricken Red. With an increasingly irritated fan base and no basic motor skills, the singer should be smashing up his instrument not playing it.

Dave Diamond

The food arrived, macrobiotic curry and chilli. It was carried from the kitchen in wide, silver dishes, by a string of hungry guests. I joined them, bulging in a semi-circle round a table under the marquee, then soon swaying out with a heaped white plate. I sat on a large tree stump on the side of the now-vacated stage.

A shaven-headed American sat down next to me, expertly disengaging his food from the plate. His mobile phone activated.

"Hi baby. Fine... Eating... Sure. You're right. There's a lot of choices in everyone's life."

He grimaced into the phone, nodding, then put his hand over the mouthpiece and looked at me, "Say, talk to my girlfriend. She needs advice."

He handed me the phone. An earnest English voice wondered from the receiver,

"I mean, do I just come back and finish my PhD when this internship with NATO is over, or do I go back to South America to work with those street children? Maybe I should just get a job in a bar and finish my novel? I don't know. I think all I want is to have six children and live by a river. Hello? Gavin?"

I handed back the phone.

"I'm here babe. I was just taking some quiet time to think seriously for you."

He listened again and continued to eat. I spotted Will and stood.

"Oh, there you are Ben. Having fun?"

"Not fun exactly Will."

"Seen Jess?"

"Not for a while."

"Sue?"

"No."

"Probably inside."

We walked towards the largest barn, ducked through a sleek wooden door into a pot-strewn kitchen, then slipped into a low corridor. Open and closed doors shuttled past as we went deeper into the barn. Will paused abruptly, then bolted up a smart curl of iron stairs. I followed and we came out into a long, dark room running the full length of the upper barn. Wide windows peered upon a tent of moonlit branches and low white lights were studded around the walls. Two computer screens emitted blankly at the far end of the room, and two figures adjusted into visibility on a sofa half-way down it. They paused their conversation. The nearest, a female, looked over towards us.

"Will. Hi. I'm just..."

"You're still working?"

"Just finishing." She turned away and spoke to the other figure. They stood and walked towards us.

"Will, this is my associate, Martijns Vebruegen of the European Commission."

The man rubbed his light suit lightly and extended a large veined paw – nails clean as crescent moons. Sue continued, "Martijns, this is my friend and neighbour Will White. And this..."

She looked at me. Will stepped in,

"Sue. Martijns. This is my friend Ben."

Sue grinned, "Will's told me about you."

There was a soft, inclusive chiding in her voice. I flapped a little.

Mr Vebruegen nodded at Sue, "Always a pleasure. Until July the 6th."

Sue confirmed the date and he excused himself in impeccable manner, disappearing in stripes down the tight stairwell.

Will nipped the tip of his thumb with his fingers, and looked at Sue, "Seen Jess?"

"Who knows where she gets to."

Sue's eyes flashed out, controlled and warm and volatile, wet with green. Her voice was flat and lulling, there were games in it and it seemed far away – her northern vowels corralled somewhere, softly within southern successes. Her hair was black and straight. It seemed almost muscular where it met her rounded shoulders. I had seen photos of her in the paper, seen her once on TV also.

"Outside? Inside?" She proffered options, then led us, "Let's stay here."

An open palm was batted gently through the air towards the sofa. Will and I walked forward and Sue followed; a charm bracelet round her ankle chuckling with each step. She sat on the floor, forming a diamond within her legs, then she pushed her skirt down to form a bowl within that. She placed the heel of one palm on the carpet at her side. There was silence and Sue smiled abstractly and looked beyond me.

"So," she pulled herself into the world, "how long are you staying with us?"

"I don't know, I only arrived yesterday."

Quickly, she turned to Will, "Still blue Will?"

"Not blue exactly. Pissed off, Sue."

"About what? Big house, rich wife, healthy lad, friends, looks... Not impotent are you? We'll be screwed when Jessie leaves you if you can't get it up."

Will looked vexed for a moment then stood, "I'm going to find her."

I flexed to my feet also. Sue nodded for me to sit. Will observed this, "Sue? Don't you think you should come to your own party?"

"It'll go all night. We'll be left with the dregs and the fun at dawn. I'll come Will."

She ushered him away with her voice, "Go and find Jess."

Sue stood and walked to the stereo. Faint wind-like music crept from the speakers. I felt uncomfortable and laughed. Sue did a small cough-giggle.

"What do you do, Ben?"

"Little. You?"

"I'm a businesswoman,"

"What is your business?"

"Computers and things. Tell me something good."

"I like your house. I used to play in this barn. It was tumbling down and we'd light fires with the beams and try and make batteries explode. I loved it here."

Her smile was warm and quick and she flicked her head upwards and moved two fingertips down across her cheek. I thought for a moment that she was crying. Clunking rose from the stairwell and the torso of Maggie Twist loomed into view.

"Time to film."

I nodded and Maggie descended. I turned to Sue, "Coming down?"

"Later."

I walked to the top of the stairs then turned,

"Sue? Do you look at yourself first in photos?"

"Why?" Then sensing the innocence of my question, sensing that I meant it as play, she answered, "Yes, always, unless... Yes, I always do."

❧

I took several paracetamol in the morning then drew a self portrait:

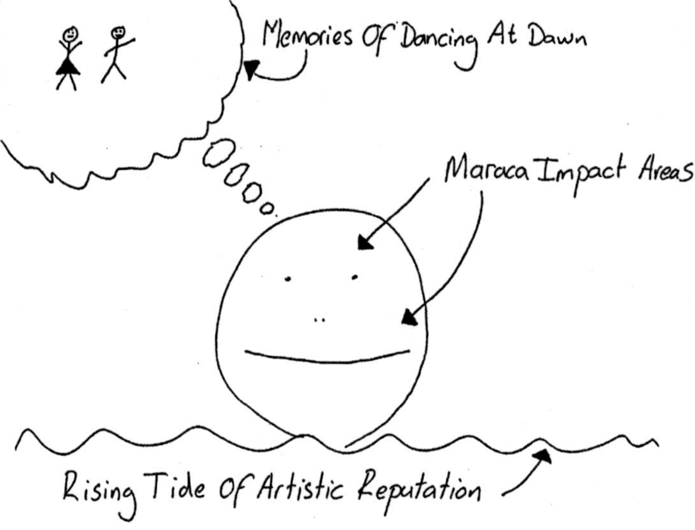

IV

Maggie was due to start work in the barn in which the three had railed against art, but a quick glance around had convinced her of the unsuitability of its light. I was taking my morning tea break when she called me at Will's.

"The light in the barn is shit."

"*Shit* Maggie?"

"Shit."

"Paint outside."

"Natural light is over. You should know that. You're going to fix it."

Two minutes later I had placed a ladder against the eaves of the barn, climbed up it and was removing roof tiles while Maggie supervised from inside the building.

"Good, good, a few more."

The hole in the roof enlarged steadily.

"Two more, from the left."

A wide beam of sunlight now fell into the barn and coated the dust kicked up by Maggie's shuffling directions. "That's it. Sunlight and darkness. Sunlight and darkness."

"What will you do when the sun moves?"

"It won't dare. Where are my sitters?"

They were late. Of course they were. Maggie herself had missed the allotted start time by over an hour, but this was forgotten within a welter of agitated preening. She called Will's house on the mobile. No answer. Pavel emerged from the far barn. He was soft and raggy from sleep and his torso loomed within a white T-shirt. Brown sandals clacked at his heels. He nodded at me and took a seat on a tree stump in the courtyard. He smoked luxuriantly and angled his face to catch the sun.

I walked back up to the house to retrieve Will and Archie. They were in the study, Will reading a story to the child, who ignored him and hurled plastic bricks against an antique globe.

"Will, Maggie's ready."

Will pointed his eyes at me. "Bloody painting."

He stood and left the room, walking towards his bedroom. I heard his brief exchange with snoozy Jess.

I waited for a while in the kitchen, then Will, Archie and myself went down to the barns. Maggie had by this time managed to lure Sue from inside the largest barn, though not entirely wean her from compact devices. Sue walked round the courtyard, connected to her mobile phone. She was talking of someone at someone else, "He's not up to it. Never has been. Get him out of there… I don't know, do it yourself. None of us have got the time. Do you want me to come over and do it? Right then, no problem."

She spotted me and ceased long enough to offer a wave. I suspected this was Sue's version of a holiday. She was wearing black jeans, shining with wash days; granular and white-threaded round the buttocks and knees. I will say no more of Sue's buttocks, though it is fair that I am permitted to think of them. The sun made her hair darker.

Chairs were brought into the barn. Maggie rejected them. Stools were brought in. Sue disliked them. Pavel helped me disengage a large sofa from the tight passageways of the house. He said nothing as we carried it. Where I had pallid hammocks of dormant flesh, Pavel had pinging, geological biceps. I wondered if he would speak. I didn't mind that he didn't though, I was comfortable with him, comfortable in his silence. The sofa proved satisfactory and was placed under the column of sunlight.

Will, Sue and Archie wrestled into comfort as Maggie arranged her equipment. She placed a large easel, then instructed Pavel to align an enormous white canvas upon it. She placed a shallow wooden box containing photos and card and plastic next to the easel, then she ferreted inside her bag to produce a pair of shades. She put them on then stood back and smiled.

Jessica arrived. She walked into the barn, her body wrapped amongst a huge bathrobe, still yawning, alluring as new-baked bread. She wore nippy white trainers and balanced a slender cup of coffee on a glossy white saucer. She offered a purring, "Morning."

"Afternoon," sniffed Will from the couch.

Sue called me over and whispered. I went upstairs to retrieve her laptop. I returned and Sue opened the machine and began to type. Maggie continued to change the placing of the easel. Jessica watched from the doorway and Pavel stood behind her, the sun rushing down to light him. Maggie became irritated, "This canvas is wrong."

She grimaced and flicked her shades up to rest within her huge hair. She paused, then abruptly, "Ben, bring me that door."

She pointed to a huge white plane of wood leaning up against the cobbled wall, its top left corner black and softened with creeping mould. I lifted it across and Pavel and I wrestled it onto Maggie's easel. "Better."

Maggie approached the sitters and stared at them. Archie was gurgling on Will's knee and Sue was typing, her forehead tense with concentration.

"Ben." Squealed Maggie, "Ben, get the camera."

A smooth aluminium box lay in the corner of the barn. I unclasped its lid and lifted out the camera, blinking into the eye-piece. Maggie walked away from the sitters and began to manoeuvre paint onto the ex-door.

I focused on Maggie, then on the globular pigments she lashed onto the door. Her shoulders popped quickly forward, poinging chubbily as she worked. I focused on the still shapes of the sitters behind her. Archie had begun to nod and slumber. Will pasted a stiff grin to his face, as though for a photograph. To Will's left sat Sue. She had stopped typing now, and as I focused on her face, the camera saw her eyes, straining down, her head facing forwards, but her eyes angled down to look at Will's hand, where it lay, palm resting atop plush cords, the dull band of his wedding ring circling and circling round one hairy finger. I heard Jessica and Pavel shift behind me.

Maggie concentrated incomprehensibly for almost one hour – sometimes painting, sometimes not – before the sitting broke up in a flurry of Archie's bowels and Sue's restlessness. The sitters were instructed to reconvene for the late afternoon, and Sue hurried off to commune with technology. Maggie, Jessica and Pavel disappeared into Sue's house, the women vocally anticipating a series of complex nouveaux cocktails. Will hoisted Archie onto his hip and walked back towards the house. I put the camera into the gleaming box and followed Will around the lake. The heat was close.

I stopped into the vegetable garden. Will halted and half-turned and looked at me, his floppy child leaning out at his side. "Not coming for lunch?"

"Haven't earned it yet."

He smiled at me, suggesting I was quaint but admirable. "Suit yourself."

I lifted the spade from the battered wheelbarrow and stepped towards a turf I had begun to lift that morning. I leaned on the spade and slid its edge into the earth. It felt strange. I made three more right-angled cuts of the earth, and lifted a limp square of turf in the spade's palm.

Each time I had punctured the earth with the spade's sharp cleat, I jolted. It was a surprise – I was affecting a change in the physical world. To lift the earth, to see it move, to see an effort correspond so directly to a result, was weird. I wasn't sure if I liked such immediacy. Where were the phone and the modem and the PC – the accoutrements necessary for modern distance doing? Not here. Just a spade that went up and down, and earth that lifted, and a filthy wheelbarrow that creaked across the lawn.

In the year of the screens, I had moved memorandums and recommendations. And I knew from the year of the screens that the bubble of communication and digital information, and the attendant edgy numerals of Dow Jones and Nikkei Dow, were real, real doing, and that they could affect the world more than this spade, for good or bad – could negligise companies and countries and lives, yet waft others upwards, ravelling them upwards in beatific affluence. I knew that. This spade seemed scanty and luddite and squalid.

But it was also true that digging had its own power, its

own reality – the jolt of actual doing pulling down the head, tempting it to find life solely in the quotidian ecology between man and earth. Man and earth – Utopia and Exile, Eden and Babylon – and still now, among the hysterical shares and information bubbles, the sentimentality of the earth was strong, always would be – excellent long term brand recognition; capable of stable trading in a bullish, fickle psyche. And to cut the earth was like breaking through a screen, changing from being projected upon to being an actor – breaking through the screen to the other side where things didn't just roll and flicker in perpetual binary anxiety, but recognisably happened.

If the year of the screens was virtual then the garden was actual. Though both were real. You could see things; banal, elementary things happening in this garden. And it was the banal and elementary that I wanted, that I needed most. The year of screens had enfolded my mind, pacifying and involuting thought, confining it as an adjunct to information.

I saw the ruddy kink of a worm and a must of earth rose to my face. I could see the blue lake at the bottom of the garden, and the warped ring of branches which wagged above and across it; the coolness of the water laying like a flat and polished stone beneath. I felt someone behind me and looked around to see Sue.

"Peasant."

I allowed myself a melancholy half-truth, "Wouldn't mind."

"Why?"

"Simplicity, connection, stability. The ground and the sky and the man between."

She sniggered, "… And poverty and boredom and marrying your sister, and backache and the same food everyday, and no decent films and all that cheap wine and bad accordion music. You sentimental tit."

She was right.

"What are you up to Sue?"

"Came to see you."

"You could be missing out on a deal."

"There'll be others."

"What are you after?"

"I wanted to watch you work. You don't get to see much work around here now my builders are on holiday. Will lies down for a week after he's lifted his fork. And Pavel, well I suspect that Pavel does his best work in dark rooms."

"He's a bit mysterious."

"It's true. I've never heard him speak."

"What's his story?"

"He turned up in Dover in the back of a meat van, came with his brothers. Maggie saw him turning tricks in Soho and paid him to model for her. He stayed with her, and they got married… They are fond of each other I think. They were in lust once, or at least Maggie was. It works. It's convenient. Marriages based on love are inconvenient."

"Has love been inconvenient for you?"

"… Continues to be." Then a moment later, "Dig or something, I want to see you work."

I turned my back and twisted the spade to break the roots. I lifted out a clod of earth and dumped it in the wheelbarrow. I could feel her behind me, twitching, wanting to talk, and I smiled to myself, feeling that she was interested in me. I'll write that again, feeling that she was interested in me. I filled the wheelbarrow and walked it over to a mound of earth that Will had designated 'landscaping materials'. My silence was making Sue want to talk, so I concentrated on digging; it was simple, predictable – this capricious wealthette was not. I enjoyed the chronic obviousness of the action:

The spade did this...

And the wheelbarrow did this...

But the girl could do this...

Or this....

This, even...

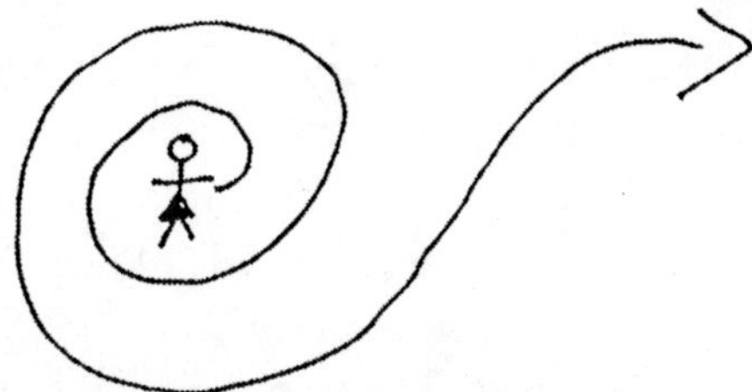

Tillers of allotments worldwide, I salute you. I see your flight from complexity of life. I understand you... A global coalition of allotment owners will rise and radically simplify...

"Stop now Ben. Talk to me."

"You wanted to watch me work?"

"I've done that, talk to me."

I sat down next to her on a ridge of earth which climbed up towards a flower bed. She was rolling a daisy stalk in her fingers and looking up to see the gleaming cross of a plane emit a long and falling trail. Her fingernails were thick and bitten and her hands were wide. They were not like her hands should be. To let me look at her she carried on looking at the sky. I saw the down and the moles beneath her chin and the acute bowl at the base of her neck. I sat in silence. I felt that she wanted to speak, wanted some words to move towards me. But she said nothing also. I looked up to the sky. It seemed like surface water which I saw from the bottom of a pool. Eventually she stood.

V

Maggie was leaving for London to finalise a show about to open at her gallery. Pavel was driving her down. She looked at me just before she left, the aluminium box of the video camera clutched in her left hand. "You'll be in the show Ben, I'll give you a credit."

She turned to Pavel. He was leaning back into the enormous white sofa, his arms stretched out, suspending Archie above his head. The boy was staring down at him, gurgling; their eyes smiling together in deep brown agreement at the pleasure of their game. Pavel eased Archie down onto the cushion, stood, uncreased his clothes and walked towards Maggie, taking the camera from her grip. They walked out.

We were in the luxurious den beneath Sue's office. She was taking the evening off. She did not want to, but Jessica's dextrous emotional blackmail had bowed her urge to work. ("We hardly see you anymore... Remember the time we drove to Barcelona... Just the girls and a bra filled with cash... No phones.") Will was there too, a little drawn and quiet, and when Pavel had relinquished the child, totally absorbed in a world of plastic tractors and primary-coloured mini-people. Jessica was in feline mode, shoes off, a long thin cotton skirt hitched up to her thighs as she stretched and drank across the furniture.

Sue sat next to me. Our sofa faced towards a huge window that ran the length of the room's back wall. Light still lingered in the sky, a clear blue falling in the West as a pure dark rose to meet it. The copse of oak curled up in the field, and the canopy nodded, black and lazy. It was a beautiful night. Sue stood suddenly and walked towards the window, pulling a lever which released it. She pushed the panels of glass to the side of the room and they folded flat against each other.

The room was open to the night. I pressed my shoulders against the sofa and turned my drink within the glass, looking at the curling flat of the field. I had always loved the fields. The emptiness of them coaxing you to think, allowing you to fill them with what you wanted… I had simulated and been stimulated in London, I had fizzed and burst with its energies – "Latest!", "Best!" And it was exciting to ride the convections and imperatives of its world streets, but the huge and empty fields did not declare or demand; they inquired perhaps. The fields allowed you in.

Sue turned the lights off in the room, so we could see more clearly the colours and darks and darknesses of the night, and she sat back down. Her arm trailed against my leg and I hoped she had intended to touch me. I felt the air change in my chest. It was going to rain. A storm now waited – in another sky still, but gathering quickly. I looked across at Jessica who was smiling in to herself, the gloss of her cheeks – Fabergé lanterns – still visible in the waning light. Perhaps I had found a new family to dysfunction within.

There was a sound of pushed fragile air and a bat whipped into the room, its radar broken or gone. Will leaned across Archie in an involuntary bolt of protection, and he looked up to the bat, following its movements with a guarded aware expression. It flitted around near the ceiling. I thought I could feel its panic. Sue watched it, motionless. Jessica raised her glass, "Another lost creature."

She laughed and then she gulped her alcohol. I imagined the spirits sliding over the wet cliff of her palate into the rapids of her throat. I was happy to see the bat. It seemed to mean something.

Will stood suddenly and lifted Archie, "I'm going to put the boy to bed. Goodnight Sue. Ben."

He leaned towards Jessica and delivered a peremptory peck onto her cheek. She did not stir. With Archie clasped in front of him, Will walked from the room. Sue watched him walk, a sadness falling onto her face. The bat dived quickly through the open window.

More drinks. More drinking. I became drunk. Jessica tried to initiate a conversation about my love life. I parried, hopefully in a way which suggested the lothario's mystique which my bad hair and strange legs did not. Jessica began to roll a joint and Sue walked to the stereo. I felt relaxed and sensual – no, honesty – I was brimming with unrealistic and disloyal sexual fantasies. Several generalised images of breasts jiggled behind my eyes... I had once slept with two women – the word slept should be taken literally – my mum's sisters on holiday on the Norfolk Broads. I was twelve and we shared the low and slanted cabin of a boat. They smelled of lotions and had papery skin. They thought I was rude. They live together in America now, the two sisters, they drink gin and bake huge pies; they take handguns with them when they go shopping.

Music crept around the room. And it was beautiful music to me, and it became more beautiful. This room, those fields, these girls – that girl in particular. And just then a deer began to bark by the lake and it sounded so clear and right. It sounded good. A good moment. There are some moments that we can always recall. They are not so different to other moments, but perhaps their importance is that we are ready to receive them. Some moments come at the right time – are in time with the life. Other moments come at the wrong time, these live in us too, they live as regret. I could see my father's face. The phone rang in another room and Sue stood and walked to answer.

Jessica untangled her legs and slowly clambered towards me. She sat right next to me. I could smell the camomile lather lifting from her boys' hair, and I saw her long nostrils open like lips for the dark night air.

"So Ben, things seem to be going well with Sue, wouldn't you say?"

"I wouldn't say anything."

"That's because you're modest. But tell me, you and I are friends."

And if we really are friends Jessica, and if you feel you can ask me anything, then why can't I ask you... 'Does Will know about you...'?

Sue came back into the room and flopped onto the couch. I looked at Jessica, her face revoked now into mask, intimacy extinguished.

"Bad news," Sue exhaled, "Jay Brockledent can't make the meeting with Martijns. Didn't sound too convincing to me..."

She leaned forward and I felt the gleam of her eyes, the playful glance rubbing across my face.

"... Ben, what are you up to next Friday? Fancy a trip to Brussels?"

Jessica entered the fray, "I'm sure we can release him for a day."

"Good. Excellent."

They smiled at each other and I opened and closed my mouth and looked out across the fields. The annoyance I felt at my days being rearranged in so capricious a manner, reached an equilibrium with the opportunity of spending time with Sue. The *possibilities* of Sue.

❧

The last time I had been with a woman... We were both drunk. Distant colleagues. It was a Thursday night. She said I was all right and she asked me out for a drink. We went to a pub whose chromium bar suggested a 1930s passenger liner. She had just split up with her boyfriend. She'd left him, "Not for *anyone* else," she said, "For everyone else." I liked that. We drank lots quickly and I paid for the cab… I threw up in her bathroom, but cleaned and apologised and laughed at myself and she decided it was okay. We did it, then sort of did it again. In the morning we phoned in sick and went out for breakfast. In the afternoon we went to see a film. It was a film about a poor young man who becomes demented. We said goodbye outside the cinema, shiftily, like vicars. I phoned a friend and went up West and got drunk. I didn't tell him everything about her. I told him some things that were true, but I made a lot of it up.

❧

After leaving Sue's, I showered against the heat and lay in bed, failing to read a novel which Jessica had thrust upon me, claiming it "defined our generation exactly, exactly". The novel was about several rich people screwing up their lives. I think her cousin wrote it. My eyes limped across the page for a while, and when I felt them bending towards the duvet, I stood and looked out of the window. After my labours, my arms were aching marginally more than my back, but I knew this was temporary and soon the back would reassert its pain preeminence.

A dark barge of cloud had taken the sky, now rain dashed and glossed against the high windows. The suit of armour was lit for a moment by the storm. It was comical in the momentary light – a photo mailed as publicity for any of many bad horror films. Then I felt sad and hollow in the darkness... A sound like a tree branch bending against the roof... The sound again. It was coming from the door, it was knocking. I climbed back into bed quickly, hoping and hoping.

The door opened and Will stood there, his boxer shorts hanging below a recently nurtured paunch. He was so white. He blinked and smiled at me. He was not the visitor I had wanted. There was fever and blankness in his eyes.

He walked across the room, and without looking at me clambered into bed. I lay completely still. Will rolled towards me and curled his leg across my knees, his arm across my chest. He placed his cheek in the nook below my shoulder and I felt his tears suddenly, falling onto my skin. He choked then, painfully – a cat retching out a warm bird's wing. I felt embarrassed, uncomfortable with skin; did not know what to say, nor what to do. I could offer him nothing except my feelings of personal discomfort and an anxious foregrounding of my latent homophobia. I stared up at the ceiling, far away as the sky and my father. Lightning lit the suit of armour and I thought again of the structure of horror: guests in dark mansions; the contrivance of hosts; nocturnal visits; the puncturing of victims, the drawing out of energy, life. Tufts of hair, risen up from his crown, tickled my cheek inappropriately.

"I should go."

He was right. But, "No, stay, try and tell me."

He sat up, the duvet falling in front of him. He brought his legs up behind him, his pose callow now, and juvenile. He looked at me, not in my eyes, but strangely just above them, and he held his gaze there. Then simply he asked, "What am I going to do?"

I had no answer to this question. It was out of my jurisdiction; it needed definition.

He captured grief in his throat, and turning its power into indignation, into the rightness of his self, he said, "Jess and Pavel."

He said it, admitted it out loud. The knowledge had escaped, multiplied. He could not go back. Will grew daring, more encumbered, crumpled, and in a whimper of shuddering relief, it all came out:

"I've known it all along. She nearly killed me at college, and it was never enough for her. I don't know what it is with her, she just needs the numbness... She's bloody reckless... She was my first. And apart from... She was my first. And I thought the baby, that Archie, I thought that having Archie would calm her down, but it hasn't. It's made her more, made her worse. She needs to prove something now... I've never caught her but I've always known. I can smell it. They say that women can smell it. Maybe I'm the woman now. People will think that I can't. God if people thought that..."

The rain calmed and the creaks of the old house moved forward.

"And what do I have? What do I have really? The boy. This house is the bank's. Jess's father pays for everything now. I've never really had Jess. Jess owns things, owns people, but she is never owned and what do I have? I'm supposed to have it all, cash, house, wife. Lucky old Will and his bloody big house and his bloody smart car and his bloody rich wife and his bloody bloody. And I could have done all that City old school thing, with the fat ties and the long lunches and meeting for squash after work. And all that cash. But can you, if you're not like that? Can you just do things because people think you will? You can't really can you? You can't go against your character, not for long, not without trouble.

"And what is my character? I feel nothing, feel like I'm waiting, rusting away. I just wanted peace with my wife and my boy. And god I'm useless. We are. What are we supposed to do? I'm like an animal, like a cow in this shitty big barn. And Jess just comes and milks me when she feels like it. And I thank her for feeling like it. And I say 'Yes Jess', and I ask her where she's been like some fucking adolescent, full of suspicion and malice and I push her away from me with jealousy. But it's not me. I never wanted this. I never wanted to share. Never wanted to hate. I should have married a bloody spastic or a pauper, then I'd have owned something, owned someone. I own that bloody boy though.

"When I wake up I just think about killing myself. Everyday I just think 'Today's the day', but I know if I get up and see the boy or that stupid fucking sun then I won't be able. So I try to hold the boy. The trees here are so beautiful. And it's all so pathetic and if I had the energy or I mattered enough I'd hate myself. I just want to stop, be over, be nothing. But the boy and the warm sun and those beautiful pines and the lake.

"And always the thought that she'll stop, that she'll stay at home, because every time she's with someone she's saying that I'm not enough. And I know I'm not enough. But she should say I am. That's love isn't it? Living with someone never being enough. I mean, how can you ever be enough for another when you haven't even got enough for yourself? And I've always loved her, she can be so kind sometimes and funny. Don't think bad of her. Because she can be so kind. And she is good to Archie. She's just spoiled, just a selfish, clever cow. She's not pathetic... She can't help it. But I should be able to. I should be able to. What is a man though? What is a man now? I should be able to stop it."

When he had exhausted himself, he fell asleep in my bed. I lay awake for a long time, then stood by the window and saw the stupid sun rise to coat the fields. I looked towards Will in the bed. There was something cruel in me as I watched him. I felt detached. His face and the morning creep of the warming sun made me bitter...

Yes, it was hard for Will. Yes, I know that pain and death and humiliation and the like are no respecters of money and position. I know we are all born into the same equation; a principle my grandmother expressed pithily: "We all piss in the same pot." I know all this. I know he's just like me.

But seeing Will lying in his parent's bed with the morning etching across the suit of armour, with his deer barking outside, and his nearby son, and that face – Will is so beautiful – I thought it was wasteful for him to live in such bleakness. It seemed rude, a miscalculation. And for him to weep and gnash, and pay hysterical nocturnal visits, did nothing to repeal the inviolable hardness of his life. It just made him look like a tit. Because if he'd had the inclination (he's certainly had the time) to stretch his thoughts and feelings away from the pain that exists, so mournfully, in his own central nervous system, he might have seen other things. He might have seen better things, worse things...

And it hurts me when you are weak Will, it hurts me. Please get better, try to be better than this, try to be better. Or your house may fall apart. Accidents may happen. Brakes will slowly skid.

east

I

Pavel took one hand from the steering wheel and wafted a small tin towards me.

"Sveet, Ben?"

I did not want a sweet, but I took one and popped it in my mouth. Pavel had spoken.

It was one week since Will had visited my room. Now Maggie, Sue, Pavel and I were heading for London, for the opening of Maggie's new show. The next day, Sue and I were heading for Brussels.

The mugginess of the day combined with the leather upholstery in Sue's huge old Citroen to stick us to the seats. Pavel's arm jolted forward periodically to flip a tape of drunken accordion music. Maggie leaned towards me so our arms were touching, "Such shitty music."

She was in a sour mood. Her painting had not gone well that week. It had been pointed out by a surly, unimpressed Will that the portrait of Archie looked like a dog, that Sue looked like Will and that Will looked like a particularly brutal security guard. Maggie had told Will to "Fuck off and sit down". Will had sat down.

Now Maggie nodded at Pavel. "He's been playing that tape since I met him. It's his uncle's, wheezing it out at some Pristina wedding. Reminds him of home I suppose."

There was something brute in her voice, a sneer which seemed to say that Pavel's life was more petty than her own. I was surprised to hear myself rising to the lothario's defence, "Does anything remind you of home Maggie?"

Without releasing me from her eyes, Maggie whisked

up her top, proudly showing an exhibit. I broke from her stare and looked at her naked breast. A round purple welt was set in her skin, an incinerated base camp, a nodule for deflating dinghies.

"One of my fathers was a careless smoker."

She pulled her arm away from mine. In that moment Maggie changed from words – cynical, opportunist, charlatan – into a person: a fully dysfunctional person, dense with ambiguity. I wanted her to touch me again. I wanted her to feel the warmth for her that grew suddenly within me. Can you ever judge another? I don't know. I will hazard an answer though: probably not. But there is a caveat – I think that sometimes you have to anyway. Probably can't, but have to anyway – not the best of deals.

The fields began to succumb to the strips of brick which courted the road, and the strips began to rise, changing from dwellings to shops, offices, multiplexes, banks, and soon we hit the East End of London. If I am forced to judge (which I can't but must do anyway) then the East had always been my favoured part of the capital, my bolt hole. There was something solid about the East that I did not find in the West of London.

The West of London moves quickly, it is future and projection, its spaces and places revolving with nuance and fashion and the undertow of the hefting imperatives of bottom line. The West is B-list faces, snorting in the mirrored toilets of private and angular bars – the bars themselves situated above discreet, ivied brasseries. West proffers sleek versions of the self to those vigorous enough to dream and spend. It is aspiration, inspiration, mobility, flexibility; it is neotenous; it is conference and lapdance and Champers and thrill. West is nippy and natty – randy as it is elusive; elusive as it is imagined.

But the East moves slowly, lumbers intractably in the grey waters of washing machines in second-generation laundrettes. East is salty pubs, fists and Sky Sports, kebab-greased armchairs. It is benefits and theft and curry pies and black and brown and trashy, pan fried white. The East is TB still and it is the cavities of factories boxing now into mono-person homes. The East is docks and strangers and space; and it is the Thames, England's mouth, opening up to taste the world – on the cheap though, always on the cheap.

If the West asked: "Where do you see yourself in five years?", the East asked: "What you up to mate? Pub? Bookies?" The West floated dreams, and I suppose the East grounded them. There was something more real for me about the East, more suited. I always felt comfortable there; less precarious – less to lose in the East, not so far to fall. Jessica is West; born West. Sue is West too; though I think she once was East. I'm East; born and bred.

One place where the East and the West met, where the West came over to the East, was the art world. Cheaper studio and gallery space, and the romantic and everlasting notion of cruddy, malnourished bohemianism located the art in the East. The West loved to slum over, to feel the edge. The East made art authentic for the West, it laundered experience into object. And when driven West, post-purchase, to the high, long Western flats; when hung on the wall to observe brunches and cocktails and infidelities, it was hoped that the art still had East on it – warehouse skylight, paint-splattered factory floor, life among the immigrants, drug-shipments nosing darkly up to shabby docks.

The West came East for art and the East lay out its palm for the cash. The East spent the cash that night, on its friends, in a late night drinking club, with maybe a bit left for a takeaway or even something for the rent, if West had really liked.

Maggie needed to be late so we parked and spent a couple of hours amongst the thick glass tankards, worn and mottled carpets and quiz machines of a local pub. Maggie also needed to be loud, so she hoovered powders off the once-white cistern and guzzled vodka Cossackly by the bar. At precisely one hour and twenty minutes beyond her expected time of arrival, we needlessly took a cab the hundred yards to the gallery.

Flashes flashed. The red lights of TV cameras pin-pointed Maggie.

"This way love, beautiful tonight", "Over here girl", "Maggie, give us a smile."

She did all of it. She did it all, and loved it, and managed to look like it was a drag. She condescended to speak into a microphone, "Yes, I think this is my best show yet. I was on the ouija board to Picasso last night and... *Ah*," her eyes trailed towards me, "have you met 'The Latest Thing'?"

She beckoned me over. The cameras and the fuss made me dumb. I went.

"This man here is my protégé, but soon, well he'll tell you how he plans to eclipse me."

She walked away from me, leaving me stranded in a puddle of TV light.

"What are you working on?", "How does it feel to be recognised at last?", "Any plans to break America?"

I blinked and felt disdain growing in my stomach,

"Look, I'm not an artist, I'm a gardener. I fix boilers as well. This is a mistake, Maggie's joke or something."

"Do you think that this modesty is an inherent part of your work?"

My disdain fractured into laughter and I saw Sue looking over at me, smirking. I thought, why not? Why not?

"Yes modesty is an inherent part of my work. All this has been an accident. My whole career was based on mistakes. I consider the modern art market to be contrived, disingenuous toss. The accident is the only way to be honest in such a climate, the random forms of the subconscious defeating the egotism of the star-based art world. I am not an artist. You are not journalists. I wouldn't know art if it mugged me. You wouldn't know news if it pissed in your pint. I'm hungry, I'm going in."

I walked towards the gallery door and noticed the earnest face of a young man, a wannabe artist I guessed, nodding at me gravely. He looked at me strongly in the eyes, and seemed to say, 'You are right, this is art.' I laughed thoroughly through the revolving doors and found myself in a large white space, dotted with perfect clothes that had brought thin people with them. I drank and lied and laughed.

I got talking to a journalist, his name was Dave Diamond, he wrote that piece on Sue's party. He seemed okay, a bit flash and slippery, but he was interesting. I told him that the art star routine was a mistake. He didn't believe me. I tripped and spilled a drink on him, but he was okay about that. Sue didn't seem to like Mr Diamond. She kept her distance when we were talking and spent time with a six-foot Chinese woman.

One of Maggie's sculptures was called *Fathers*:

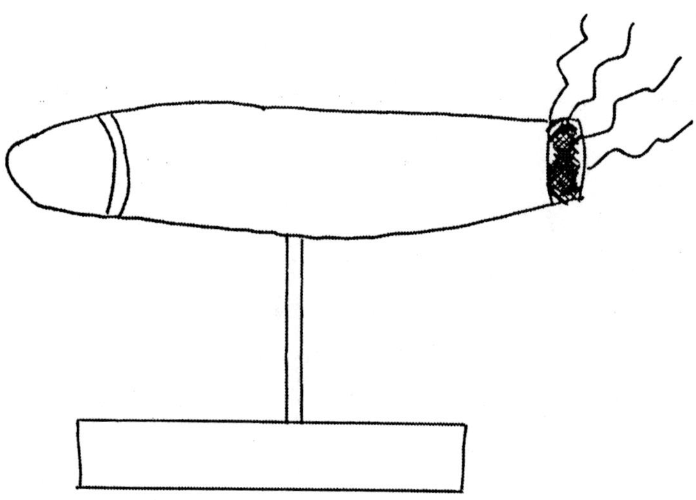

II

There were several hours available between waking with a hangover in Maggie's apartment and catching the train to Brussels. These were hours in which Sue did not intend to not consume. With huge speed we were among cabs and bags and slender sales assistants compelled into fawning imbecilities by the depth and colour of Sue's plastic. I was, I confess, moody and sweating with the previous night's intake, and perturbed by Sue's brash, compulsive shopping. I was uncomfortable with the velocity of her drive to own.

But in a way I liked it, liked the lack of restraint. I had never seen her so girlish. She was rendered eleven years old by retailing excitement. Sue was thrilled by the textures of cloth and the colour of hat, and the shape of shoes. She was genuinely thrilled. I followed her like a golem, with less surface avidity than the assistants, but in my own way, I was perhaps the greater predator. I sat on a chair outside the someteenth changing room and waited for her. Sue stepped out of the cubicle and walked towards the cash desk. She dropped a small white dress onto the counter. The assistant slid Sue's plastic through the approving groove. Two minutes later we stood on the street looking for a taxi.

The door slotted firmly into the sleek bubble of the new black cab and she leaned back, balancing a herd of bags across her legs, "Thanks for waiting. I could see that you disapproved. But it's your turn now. Let's see how shallow you get."

Minutes later, the cab pulled into Savile Row. We stepped out and towards a shop and I eyed its silvered mirrors and wooden veneers. Sue pulled me inside. A middle-aged man smiled at us in feudal supplication, "Sir?"

"He'd like three suits. Off the peg unfortunately, we need them today."

Soon I was aping the crucifixion as the servile tailor wrapped me in measurements.

"He'd like one classic. A pin-striped something. And one summer suit, light and crisp. A Chardonnay of a suit. You choose the third."

The tailor nodded at the lady and scurrying shop assistants materialised and assumed different trajectories towards distant areas of the shop. They returned quickly and silently with several appropriate suits, which they hung on a clothes rail by the high, oak cash desk. They promptly disappeared.

I retired to the changing rooms and slipped into a double-breasted city pin stripe. As I looked in the mirror I felt a change. I fingered the lapel of the suit. The material was rich and firm and soft, it hung perfectly from my skinny shoulders. My legs no longer appeared odd. An emotion which ten minutes before I would have called vanity, or a capitulation to decadence, surfaced, and I now labelled it pride: pride in one's appearance. The quality of the cloth was having a mind-altering effect. It was a psychotropic suit.

I tried on several more suits and twisted and turned in front of Sue, now installed in a crinkled brown leather sofa, sipping a Bloody Mary procured by an assistant from a nearby restaurant. The smile on my face became less suppressed.

In the cab she teased me, "You fell in love with yourself in there."

I was puzzled. "I may have."

"It's about time."

We deposited excess bags at one of Sue's trusted hotels, then drove to Waterloo station. I had bought an afternoon paper on the trot between retail spaces and now I leaned back and pulled it from my pocket. Page seven caught my attention:

TWIST ECLIPSED BY 'ACCIDENTS AND MODESTY'

THE CREAM OF the globe's arterati flocked last night to East London's hip Salary Gallery for the opening of Constable Prize-winner Maggie Twist's new show, Brazen Knacker. The show featured works in keeping with Twist's *oeuvre* to date – a naked cellist bowing his pubic hair in the entrance hall – but it also marked an enigmatic departure for the Essex impresario. *Wishing Well* – a bucket of the artist's own urine with authentic Roman coins tossed to its bottom – flowed in a direction which Twist is calling her 'Water Sports' work.

Despite the smell of Twist's offerings, the critics reached rare agreement that the real star of the night was her young protégé, whose earnest outburst on arriving at the gallery looks set to instigate a new direction in British art. While Twist's consistently revolting work commands lucrative loyalty among the hoovers and breakers of the art world, a sky-high rise is predicted for the young star with the simian forehead, who styles his métier 'Accidents and Modesty'.

I was able to spend a few moments with the in-demand artist, and asked him to elaborate his manifesto. At first he would not be drawn, saying, "I don't have one." But several champagne cocktails later, he deigned to offer a manifesto in action rather than the dry, theoretical proclamations which he evidently feels so limit his work. The artist/gardener spilled his drink on me in a perfectly hoaxed accident, then apologised profusely, managing to look genuinely modest.

As the artist left the gallery, a fist-fight erupted between truck-jawed socialite Jay Brockledent, and opiated singer Danni Red, formerly of the platinum-selling rock band Mudfugger.

While kangaroo canapés circulated, gurning Red utilised Twist's sculpture *Sharp Pie* on the exposed shoulder of the recently redundant Brockledent. The fight spilled from the gallery into the gutter, forcing the artist/gardener, and his consort, the cheaply-dressed e-stess Sue Watson, to modestly step over the groaning pugilists into a waiting cab.

This surely is a young man beyond the public relations, false hysteria and amateur journalism of today's art world; a man who refuses to talk the flashy talk, refuses even to walk the trashy walk, but prefers instead to walk the zashy walk. Expect great things.

III

We walked beneath the elongated bubble of the Eurostar terminal and entered the first class carriage. A man with a laptop looked at us long enough to be unfriendly then continued to read. We found our seats. They were wide and wrapped in thick burgundy cotton. There were some buttons in the arm and an extendable tray which I manoeuvred. Sue perched tensely within the seat. The train moved out of the station and juddered a wide arc into South London. A waitress arrived. Sue began to speak to her in French, which seemed to be her native language, but the waitress smiled at Sue in a way suggesting the mispronunciation of certain Gallic vowels, and replied in English. An announcement in Flemish filled the train.

A bottle of champagne breached the confusion. The cork tumbled down the aisle, falling to rest against the sliding door at the end of the carriage. We aimed to get drunk. By the time the train had left London and slid to a temporary halt at Ashford, we had more or less achieved this.

I had never travelled on the Eurostar before, never been to Belgium either. When I arrived I would be an Englishman. In England I was rarely knowingly an Englishman, the categories of identity used at home being much smaller: "He's from the East, Suffolk. His dad killed himself." That sort of thing. Soon I would be English. I ripped straight into my bag of clichés, activating my chauvinism by asking Sue if she could name six famous Belgians – she named nine, tossing in the inventor of the saxophone, and a famous 'French' singer with an American name.

Then she said, "Bastard. 'Cheaply dressed'?"

"What?"

"That *bastard* Dave Diamond or whatever he calls himself, saying I was cheaply dressed. He's so bitter."

"About what?"

"Our divorce."

Sue expanded, "He was living here when I met him. He one who made me aware of all this lucrative corruption. He was called Tom then, and was an angel, an earnest crusader. He was an investigative journalist, a brilliant one."

The windows plunged into darkness as the train entered the tunnel.

"He came to stay with me a lot when I was blagging money out of the City, and he just got diseased, gave up the tough work, and got into celebrity journalism. He stalks the country now with his paparazzi henchman, waiting for pop stars to fart."

"What happened?"

"Different things."

"Why did you split up?"

"I left him."

"Why?"

"Have a drink Ben."

It was a good idea. I was interested in a lot of booze being inside me. I drained the bottle of wet fizz. Sue ordered another. I was keen on that also. The windows flickered into light and the train began to increase in speed. I looked at Sue, my mind torpid and slow as it digested, tried to digest the thought of a married Sue.

"Did you wear white?"

"Leave it for a while and you might get what you want. We have to prepare."

She pulled a piece of paper from the bag beneath her seat, and began to write down the essentials for my behaviour at the coming meeting. She made me repeat the main contours of my actions out loud, then made me repeat them a few minutes later without the paper in front of me. It was difficult to be serious with the booze cracking in my veins and this beautiful woman, the ex Mrs Diamond at my side. But serious she wanted and serious I was... I bet she did wear white. I bet she did. Would did do, I do I do I do.

❧

At Gare Du Midi I got another glimpse of Sue. We'd had Sue the rustic hippy, Sue the entrepreneur, Sue the consumer, Sue the once-married, now we got Sue the sentimental lover of public transport. She had achieved a bloating of the purse via a foreign exchange transaction, and was now heading to the tram stop. Yes, she said, we could obviously afford a cab; and yes, it would be much quicker; but yes, she said, she still wanted to take a tram. She liked the way they wobbled and groaned, and she liked the tram's bell. On the choice between taxi and tram, I did not care. I wanted Sue to do whatever made her more Sue.

We sat down in the tram, facing each other on battered grey seats, our knees almost touching. And the tram did wobble and it did groan. It pondered and slopped round the slow uphill corners. The bell rang also; twice, once inexplicably, and once in frustration at a woman with a kitten-sized dog whose oblivious approach to traffic threatened to halt us. We climbed a long, slow slope and I looked out of the window. Three and four storey houses lined the road, fruit sellers and bars bursting from their feet, and higher, the grey stone was fume grey also. We came into a square, its centre dominated by a solidly ostentatious civic building – crests and turrets and wide steps announcing its centrality to the life of the polity.

We passed to the left of the building down a thin commercial street of computer shops and restaurants and hardware sellers. The air was warm and close and the late afternoon sun was fugging through grey clouds and making them light – still grey, but light, really light. I had never seen really light light grey light before. It puzzled me, refuting other light I had seen. If you have seen this light, I would like to know. Maybe you can explain it, maybe we can talk about it?... I welcome more conversations on light in general: on urban neon light which dapples crouching puddles; on this Belgian light which hangs and hangs like oil paint; on the light which streams onto canvas and joins with the eye; and on the village light – that soft hive of light now falling down onto Jessica and Will.

We climbed down from the tram into a rounded place, ringed by restaurants and jolly bars. A large, brown church stood in the centre, its body high and boxy, but its front curling brazenly with Baroque effort. It looked wrong. I paused Sue and we walked around the church. There was a thick iron plaque on the front of the church. It told us that the front was built elsewhere in 1620, then moved here when the back was done in 1895. Architecture in Brussels seemed to have lapsed between these dates.

Sue said the city was "full of things like that".

"Full of things like what?"

"Like that. Weirdly beautiful screwed up things."

She told me that there had been a river in Brussels, but it had grown dirty and they'd bricked it up.

"Why didn't they clean it?"

"I don't know, too dirty maybe. If everything's dirty, what do you clean things with?"

That seemed fair. She said that there was still a canal and pointed at the confused brown church. "It's that colour."

The light had begun to detach itself from the grey and become the white or yellow colour with which I normally associate it. The sun gave a hopeful burst and the cobbles grew warmer. I carried Sue's heavy bag while she removed one of her tops. She didn't gesture to take the bag back so I carried it down the street. We walked for a minute down a wide street lined with tall, curling art deco houses. There was a staggering amount of dog shit on the pavements. I was curious about this high level of street fouling.

"Why is there so much dog shit Sue?"

"People don't like shit in their gardens."

We entered a square. It had a car park in its centre and was lined by trees. There was a gym on the far side of the square. A sign in its window declared that it had been used by one of the famous Belgians that Sue had mentioned. He was an actor apparently. Sue said that he couldn't act but that he was very good at karate. She added that I should know who he was. I had never heard of him. There may not be many karate movies featuring bad Belgian actors available in India or Queensland. Though there may be other reasons why I had not heard of him.

We paused in front of a bar, its white plastic tables and chairs falling out onto the pavement and enabling drinkers to chat in the sun. Next to the bar was a high green door, parallel lines of post boxes flapping within it. Sue delved into her handbag and after a few moments produced keys.

"My friend Isabelle's flat, she's in Frankfurt, on business."

She pushed the door open and it wafted backwards like a butler's hand. I walked inside, up the marble staircase to the first doors.

"Next floor," instructed Sue.

I heard the green door bellow shut below me. The ceilings in the house were high and some light grey light crouched in the corners of the hallways. I waited for Sue outside a white door on the next floor. She twisted the key and the door burped across a wooden floor and opened into a small kitchen. A lounge was next door. Its ceiling was ornate and high. I could have stood on my own head in the room and still had to stretch to reach the plaster. Plants threaded around trinkets and photo frames and a sheet of window peered across a wrought iron terrace into the square. I spotted a plump woman with gaudy make-up urging her shoe-sized dog to fertilise a tree. I pointed her out to Sue. Filled with the irresponsibility of travel and the masculine urge to impress, I opened the window shouting "*Fait le merde chez vous*" into the square.

I was quite proud of my French. Sue understood it, though the dog shit-enabling woman did not. My French seemed to be the type comprehensible only to the

English. That seemed fair. It had been taught to me by an English woman at school. Her name was Mrs Dawson, Mademoiselle Dawson to please her. She drove a 2CV and smoked a lot of fags. She wanted to be French. I sat with my friend Paul in her class. Paul said he'd had an affair with her. But the affair existed only in his mind. Paul wanted to have an affair with her because he said she was "nearly French". And he said that "everyone knows how much the French do it".

Paul would have known about the bad-acting karate actor. He wouldn't have known about the light grey light though. Paul's in jail now. I saw it in the local paper when it plopped through the letterbox at Will's. Paul held up a juggernaut with a piece of wood that looked like a gun. When we were at school he set fire to the cricket pavilion and was expelled though not, at that time, imprisoned. In retrospect, Mademoiselle Dawson's favours might have calmed him, curbed his pyromania; or the non-actor could have trained him to channel his aggression with the aid of martial arts. Maybe. I don't think you'd have liked Paul. Paul was difficult to like. He was intent on everything being "shit".

Another high room backed off the lounge. It was a bedroom and it led to a long, white bathroom. There was evidently only one bedroom, and evidently only one bed. It was a very big bed, plump of duvet and pillow. I tried not to look at the bed in the way that I wanted to look at it; tried also not to look at Sue in the way that I wanted to look at her. Sue caught me not looking like I wanted to look and looked at me. Sue could look just like she wanted to look. She gave me a tight, quick smile. The smile said, "Don't assume anything", "There's still some way to go", "I am able to check into any hotel in the world at short notice". I put the suitcase down and sat down in the lounge. I judged that the length of the sofa was just shorter than my own body.

As Sue changed, I walked around the flat, opening things and lifting things up. I suspended my wait for Sue between speculation on the character of the flat owner and gulps of tea. I liked the woman who lived there. I liked Isabelle. She had glamorous dresses and frumpy mauve slippers. This implied a breadth of character. There were lots of photos of tanned young people, drinking in different hotels and restaurants and countries. I did not look in Isabelle's drawers.

Sue yielded the bathroom. We were both pleased by the way she looked in her white dress. I changed into my new linen suit. I smoothed it across my chest and scraped my hair down to de-simian my forehead. I did actually look good.

We left the flat and walked the streets around the square, idling before our restaurant meeting. Dusk was falling, falling down. I will try again with the light. A last light lay across white houses on the far side of the street. It was orange now. It looked solid, looked like you could eat it and feel warmed and better. It was the porridge of light. The paint crumbled off the wall in oaten shapes. The sky was huge and like a dream. It rolled out, cloudily under itself, until it joined I suppose, all other sky everywhere… But riddle me this. Why did the sky have to be so big? There were only little people under it. What could they do with something that big?

❧

I did look in Isabelle's drawers. Her knickers were white. Clean, sporty, sensible. As I say, I like Isabelle…

❧

The restaurant was not far from the flat; meaning that, come the return, the flat would not be far from the restaurant. Come the return. The restaurant had a deliberately shabby exterior – pokey and dark and set back – exposed as false modesty when confronted by the candelabras, inch-deep crenellations of fabric, and sumptuous low-keyness of the interior.

Is it good policy for the waiting staff to outdress the clients? Sue didn't think so, you could tell that. But I thought the waitress looked good. Her dress was a little whiter and a little more shimmery than Sue's. Sue did French with her for a while and we contrived a path through stable-like darkness towards a discreet and cunning booth deep inside the restaurant. Sue ordered an esoteric wine as we lurched into the verdant upholstery.

"Know what you're doing Ben?"

"I say little and study everything. I should be polite and clean and a little edgy. I should make Martijns wonder why you have brought me and perhaps intimidate him."

"Good. And the fourth guest?"

"Kelly. Martijns' fiancée, business partner, and secretary. I should flirt with her."

The wine came. It was not your grabbed-at-the-off-licence-on-your-way-round-your-mate's sort of beverage. I could taste the sun and the hills in it, all the old earths.

Martijns arrived with Kelly. They looked very big. Martijns seemed to be big all over, but Kelly's bigness located mostly around her head. It was her hair really. She had very big hair. If her hair were crumpled into a roughly oval shape, it would have been considerably larger than her head. Not that she had a small head. Her face had roughly the surface area of one of Martijn's palms. I stood up and shook his hand. He had sportsman's hands. He had sportsman's eyes too – a sportsman who is hearty and knows all the rules, but reserves the right to break them. Either for satisfaction or to win.

Kelly had nice hands. They were thin and clean. A little clammy with creams and cleanliness, and a little underused, but nice. They were not the hands of a busy person. I kissed her knuckle and said "*Enchanté*". I'd seen one of the Three Musketeers do that in a film. The serious clever one. The one that looked like he had something to hide; a secret love or syphilis. I could feel Sue smirking behind me, but I think she liked it. Kelly thought it was good too.

We all sat down and smiled and twitched a bit. A new waitress, this one taller, also dressed for an opulent drunken ball, added wine to the newcomers' glasses. The menus arrived. They resembled four copies of the Magna Carta – epic string-tied calligraphy detailing arcane process. Martijns began to discuss the menu with Sue in French but Sue interrupted him,

"My colleague would prefer it if our time together tonight passed in English. He is new to diplomacy."

Martijns liked this. He was grateful for the opportunity to condescend. He smiled at me, his polyglot mouth resplendent with sturdy teeth.

"... Or we can take the meeting in Hungarian, or Portuguese, or Gaelic," Sue added, "All of which he speaks."

I didn't speak a word. But neither did Martijns, I hoped.

"No, English is fine. Of course, English."

Diplomatic equality was restored.

"So Ben," Martijns ensnared me with his expensive face, "how do you feel about this investment? Do you think it will benefit Europe?"

"I have no doubt that our organisation offers an efficient method of promoting EU policy aims."

"And what of the citizens Ben?"

"We all seem well Martijns, we all seem well."

Martijns began to laugh. Kelly followed. Sue was a little concerned that I had extended my remit for the evening, but then she exhaled and I was in.

Martijns relaxed now and began to speak directly to Sue. I chatted to Kelly about the things I thought she might like. I was patronising for a bit. But she didn't like a lot of the things I thought she would. Kelly did not like sunbathing, American films, meat, swearing of any kind, cities or dishonesty. I had fun with Kelly. She ate a lot of food. I forgot that I was supposed to be lending an eagle ear to Sue's conversation. They didn't seem to care.

Glasses and plates criss-crossed the table. Somewhere in there, around the time that the things I was putting in my mouth became more sweet than before, I saw an envelope move across the table towards Martijns. The envelope seemed plump with money – plump as the pillows on Isabelle's bed. I tried not to see it, and dived back into the story about Kelly's brother's divorce. They didn't have children but there was unpleasantness about the ownership of a German Shepherd. And somewhere else in there, just as the sweet things had stopped and bitter things like coffee and cigarettes materialised, I spotted something which pleased me immeasurably. Kelly was leaning down to put something in her bag, and a painting that her marvellously solid hair had previously obscured, came into view.

It was an original painting by my friend Donald Birkin. He'd done it when we were in Queensland together, before he went to America. It was an abstract piece, less abstract than his early work though – it actually sought to depict something. It was a painting of Berlin in 1946, when it was sliced by the Allies into four sections – American, French, Russian, British. It was Berlin before the airlift but after the Reich.

Here it is:

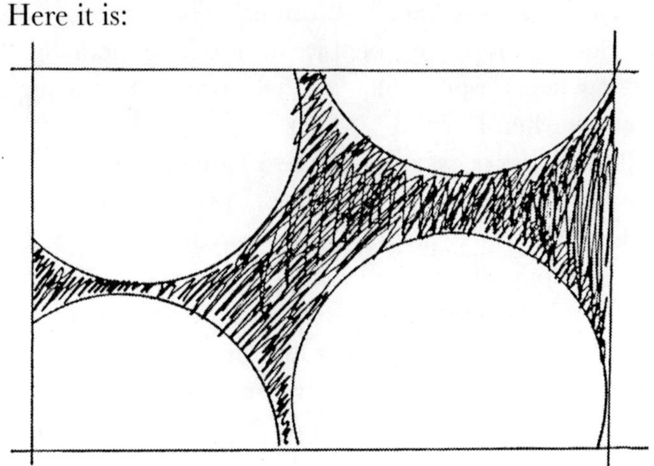

It's better than that, though.

I had an urge. A drunken urge. You probably get them. I excused myself and went to the toilet with Sue's mobile. I called Will's house and let the phone ring. A sleepy Will eventually made it to the receiver. I asked that he go to my room, locate my scraggy address book, thumb through it and give me Donald's number. Will was grumpy at first, but he was nice about it when I explained.

"I hope you get to speak to him."

"Thanks. Thanks Will."

Dialling. Drunkenness. Dialling. Donald!

"Donald, it's Ben, Ben from Queensland."

Donald was pleased and not at all surprised.

"Donald, I'm in a restaurant in Brussels with dodgy rich people. There's one of your paintings on the wall."

"Which one?"

"*Berlin 1946*."

"Good. Listen Ben, bad timing. There are people at the door. There are people everywhere actually. I'm coming to Europe soon. Just call me soon and we can meet up when I arrive."

It was always great to speak to Donald.

Kelly's hair was still absent from my view as I returned to the table. She was powdering maybe. I thought about Donald's painting while I waited for her. Like Berlin, the dinner table could be divided into four main sections – with a no man's land for salt and pepper and the like. In my painting I would depart further from the abstract than Donald and include small explanations of my suspiciously allied powers.

Like so:

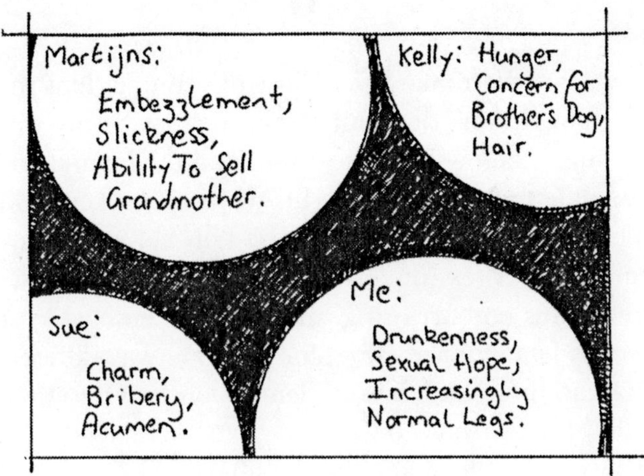

I began to listen to Sue and Martijns' conversation. Martijns was outlining some of the technicalities involved in releasing a slice of Commission funding to one of Sue's businesses. Kelly came back. Then quickly – with handshakes and small jokes which both pertly rounded off the evening and archly pointed towards future dealings; with money for the bill theatrically proffered and diligently refused; and with Kelly's hair ever so voluminously present – the evening broke up.

Outside, we laughed and waved and Kelly tottered down the cobbles, armed with Martijns, his sporting hand halting a passing taxi. Sue and I walked to the flat, meandered back.

IV

And yes we did make love. I lost my contact lens in her pubic hair. It was different to the time with my distant colleague – the night of the vomit and the liner-style bar. It was different too to the nights with my Australian. Her name was Betsy and she had moles on her stomach. But it's all more or less the same stuff, I know that now, just more or less embarrassing, more or less enjoyable. This time was less embarrassing, for me. Sue was different to how I had thought, less confident. She wanted to though, she did. I know that now.

I awoke in the night, awoke afterwards, and blinked my way into the light grey light. I focused and saw Sue above me, Sue looking down, her hair falling in front of her face. I moved my head in the pillow but still could not see her eyes. I felt a tear though, as it rolled across my shoulder. The ceiling was like the sky and the room was like the night. There were no stars. Just her hidden face like a hidden moon. Here are some of the things that Sue said that night:

"I'm sorry I thought we might be together. I did. But when I closed my eyes..."

"He doesn't even know."

"I could never betray her... I don't think I could."

"I've loved him for so long. I got married to shake him."

"I'm sorry, I thought it might work between us, I wanted it to."

"When I first met him he was such a boy. So naive and polished. Correct, but sloppy and lank, like a willow or something. He had... I don't know what he had, maybe nothing. He's sadder now, mouldier, like a grumpy cheese. I love him more now."

"I bought the barns to be near him. The barns are a trap. The portrait's a trap too – 'Sit next to me Will' – And I knew about Jess and Pavel, thought he might actually notice if they fucked in his bed. God I wish I didn't love her. And why do I? She's the bloody trap."

"Ben I'm sorry. Ben I'm sorry. It's just Will. You were good. I liked it, honestly. I thought that. It's just Will."

"And sometimes I think that I don't even like him."

Donald did another painting of Berlin. This one showed the city in 1960. The wall was up by then – *heave ho.* This phase of Donald's work seems more appropriate to this point in the story.

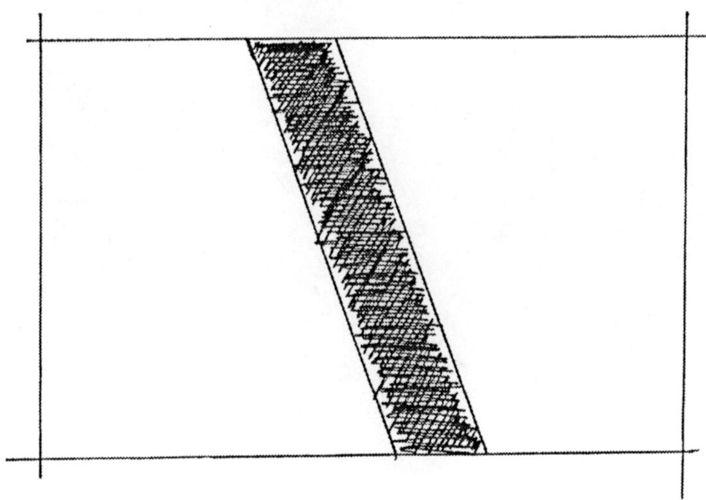

Sue is West and I am East.

Will's a wall.

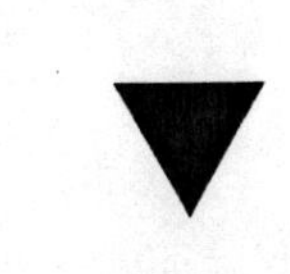

I

The weather had broken when we returned from Brussels. Summer rain sprang free latent fungi – mould on tree trunks prospered, and the implacably damp wall in the small washing room off the kitchen began to germinate spores. The light was dark grey. I fitted in with the rain, I was happy to be among it. The boredom of high damp rooms and thwarted activities found an apt corollary in my Sue'd-up heart. If someone had suggested we play Scrabble I would have agreed, 'Yes!', I would have said, 'Scrabble!' Really. I was ripe and eager for tedium. The rain slopped through the hole in the barn roof, and the painting moved under the yellow party marquee, still standing in Sue's courtyard. Had the summer ended, or just paused? Impossible to say.

Now the boiler was fixed. A week of grimy hands and the twisting of the body into painful positions to access the lumbering innards of the vast heating beast. Long mornings of deciphering the archaic engineering manual and re-glossing its fluffy corners with greased and metal-cut fingers. Heat poured from the boiler into the wall's pipes. It was a shame that it was summer and the boiler was not needed. It was a shame that the boiler would be closed down until the browning of the leaves called for its use. This immediate redundancy did not entirely deflate my feeling of pride however; I had fixed it.

I wanted Sue to know of my achievement, I wanted to tell her, wanted to say, 'Sue. I have fixed. I have demonstrated mastery over the mechanical world. I am capable Sue. Look Sue. Look. I can.'

The rain brought out a domestic side of Jessica. It

seemed to age and solidify her. She seemed static now in the big old house. She made no forays to London; made no furtive phone calls, whispering on the arm of a high chair to which the phone's cable could just extend. Jessica tutted and sighed and brewed warm beverages. A triangle of empathetic vexation, seated slightly above her nose, proclaimed the welfare of others as her goal. One morning, I came down to see her strapped round by a red cotton apron which was flaky with flour. Below the apron were large green wellingtons. I fell in love with her a bit then, a little bit. I was pleased with the way her goose-bumped calf sloshed in the wideness of her rubber boot. Jessica employed cod meteorology culled from weather reports – she said "cold front" and "not isolated showers" and the rain came down.

Jessica and I sat in Will's study and drank gin. Will was out in the garden. He had not heard the bark of a particular, juvenile deer for some nights and was concerned. He was visible from the study window in the dark grey light. The rain was tapping onto the wax of his jacket, his hands were sunk deep in the pockets of his jumbo cords, and his left ear was lifted slightly, the angle designed to capture the sound of a twig bending back across deer flank, or hooves twisting in moccasins of grass.

Jessica spoke, "I do love him you know."

"You married him."

"You must know about me, you're a listener. Discreet though, thank you."

"I do know. Will knows too."

"Oh God, he's always known. I've been doing it for years."

"Why?"

"You know why Ben. Taking someone's clothes off for the first time. It's a very spiritual thing."

"Why doesn't he do anything?"

"What can he do? Beat me? Leave me?" She laughed.

"Why don't you stop it?"

"I couldn't."

"What would you do if he fell for someone."

"I'd probably be relieved. It would be good for him. It'd get him away from Damage. That's his name for me you know? '*Damage*'. He calls me that sometimes when we're alone."

My mother came back… Alright mum? I went to see her the evening she returned. She looked like somebody else's mother. She had a tan, and the corollary of white-seeming teeth. She was full of new excitements – she had looked into the burning emptiness of the Grand Canyon. And had lost the little melon-slice of fat which had previously doubled her chin. She put her laundry on and we sat out on the little bench in the back garden. The lawn had grown less clipped. The eaves of the house leaned over, protecting us from the rain. Later we noticed that the washing machine had spewed foamy water across the orange linoleum. I fixed it.

I'd bought a bird box as a present, and I put it up in the garden at dusk. I liked hammering the nail into the wooden post. The wood was pulpy and soft and I enjoyed the sound when I hit the nail head on. I enjoyed also the lightness of the rain on my face. We sat together on the bench again, the tips of my white trainers grey from the grass' moisture. We looked at the bird box. Mother did not mention father. No need. Father was the house. As much as her anyway.

I spent the whole of the next day with her. She was happy to get back into her car. She changed the pine-scented odour eater that hung from the rear-view mirror. She bought alfalfa sprouts as well as carrots when we went to the supermarket, said she was "Trying new things". I waited for her while she had her hair done. It made me uncomfortable to see her new demi-wave. Her hair was curly now, she had widow's highlights. In the afternoon it stopped raining and we went for a walk. We roved miles, returning with our boots thick with stuck brown earth. She put all father's racing papers in the bin and I wheeled it up the drive. The bin had the house number painted on it in big white letters on the back. It was like a terrible sportsman. Mother had become a person now, that was the strangest thing of all.

I avoided Sue. She knew why. Or perhaps she didn't even notice; perhaps she thought that she was avoiding me. Jessica and Pavel did their Jessica and Pavel thing. Will sat for the painting, he cuddled Archie, he hovered around me when I weeded in the garden. "How was Brussels?" he asked once in jocular, prurient manner. He nodded off in the greenhouse with the radio on and a pot of tea, cold on a tray by his feet. He developed a fanatical interest in the English cricket tour and rushed into the garden to tell me of the fall of significant wickets. Will did everything but the things he needed to.

II

Three People Who Love Jessica was nearly completed, and Maggie wanted me to apply my rough-grained video techniques to the final session. She'd asked me to do one other thing, a film of my own. "I don't know," she said when I asked her what she wanted. "Just stumble about. Talk about things that are pissing you off."

Archie was stretched out across his father's lap, asleep, as long as a dead hare. Sue was next to Will on the sofa, her body locked stiff, miserly with eye contact. Jessica was there to witness the end of the painting, and Pavel too was beneath the marquee. He was sat on a chair by Maggie's easel. Pavel looked at Jessica, his face unable to disguise his thoughts. I hovered around the edges, filming badly.

The huge moulding door was thick with paint now, depicting cellular structures which may or may not have had limbs. Maggie demanded a break, claiming, not for the first time that day, that she was "creatively neutral right now".

Will oozed the sleeping Archie from his lap and walked around to face the canvas. I continued to film, zooming in on his face. He looked at the picture one way. He changed the angle of his head and looked at it another. He pursed his lips and bit them. He seemed agitated, confused by the work. Maggie stood near to him, rolling fingertip circles around her temples. Will's face crumpled and he decided, in lieu of addressing his real problems, to criticise Maggie.

"Do you really think that Jessica wants this?" he blurted. "Do you really think that those amoeba, or whatever they are, look like any of us, or that Jess will look at that when she's old and think, 'My lovely family, my lovely friend'?"

"I couldn't give a shit what Jessica thinks, Sue's paying..."

"Right," said Sue, pausing from typing on the sofa. "Can we get this finished please?"

"Sue's paying," continued Maggie, "and she likes it."

"I don't like it Maggie. I think it's terrible. You're the biggest charlatan I've ever met… I'll pay you more if you get it finished in the next ten minutes."

"Fuck you too then. Jessica likes it."

"I don't Maggie," chimed in Jessica, who stood behind Will now, staring queerly at the picture, "I think it's awful. Get it done girl. Put us out of our misery."

"Right then," said Maggie, pointing at the sofa, to indicate that Will should return. She approached the door. I focused on the painting.

Maggie swiftly painted a large penis swooping upwards out from the Sue-based figure's ear. Then she produced a small photograph from a number of items she kept in her box of collage materials, and nailed it squarely onto the Will-based figure's cheek. I zoomed in. It was a passport photo of Pavel.

"I'm done. There you go. 'Happy Birthday to you. Habby Thirbday dear Jessica.' I'm going to my room. Bring up my cash. And Ben don't forget the tape. I'm going to London in the morning."

Maggie turned to Pavel, "I assume you'll be staying here?"

Pavel looked at the ground and lit a cigarette.

I zoomed in on Will. His face was hard to take, it was

puce. He was staring at Pavel, hating him silently. Will glanced at Sue, waiting for her to speak, waiting for her to say, 'I think it's time you left Pavel.' But she said nothing. Of course Sue wanted Pavel to stay. Pavel could move in as far as Sue was concerned, he could drown Jessica in his semen. I looked at Will, at his anger and his blankness. Why didn't Will do something? Why didn't he do something? Why didn't anyone do anything? Why didn't I?

❧

In the early evening I laced up my walking boots and headed away from the house. I did not wish that night to maintain mother's house, nor hear Will's analysis of the finer irrelevancies of the day's play, as he audibly whirred and shuddered with impotence and hatred. I needed to be alone, needed to be quiet in the nodding green. I predicted a long and cleansing walk. I got as far as the pub.

The three beers which I swiftly drank were designed as nourishment before I continued with my walk, but they proved to be invisibly connected to three vodka and tonics, themselves connected to four large brandies. I was alone in the bar and I listened to the TV speak to itself and the quiz machine emit rhetorical queries. I walked from my bar stool to the toilet on three or four occasions. Also, I delved into the corner of a packet of crisps.

I returned to Will's house to find it dark and booming with silence. The silver aluminium box of the video camera was placed outside my bedroom door with a note attached to it. It was from Maggie and it exhorted me to film. I was drunk…

I padded down the softly arced staircase and stopped in the hallway to fix a sturdy drink. Then I walked out into the grounds with my glass and sat in the walled garden on the rotten wooden bench. The night was warm and the stars shone like liquid Christmas. A breeze pushed through the garden. It was beautiful. But I felt so drunk, and I felt so lost…

Will and Sue and Jess and Maggie and Pavel, and light and choice and chance and money and love…

I lay the camera in my lap, its lens pointing to my face. The dusty taste of frustration rose into my mouth. I pressed Record – the small red light on the camera's top my only witness. I lifted up my glass:

Half-full or half-empty?
It is not a glass, but a hovering association of paradoxically-travelling particles.
Do you lead a healthy sex life?
I have little sex in the outside world.
How long have you felt like this?
Felt like what?
Don't you think your answers have been a little defensive?
Stop having a go at me then. We need better questions.

I stood now and the camera fell and bounced into the long grass. I took a glug from the glass and looked up to the sky. My eyes followed a single cloud, lumpy as a rhino's ghost as it moved towards the moon. Then rapidly, telegraphically, my head cleared… Sue had been possibility to me, sheer possibility. We could have been. But I could not pretend her rejection, her confusion, had destroyed me. I liked her, perhaps I loved her, I felt her distance from me as a contraction. Had she broken my heart? Yes, but: broken/healed, broken/healed, broken/healed. It had happened before, Sue had merely furred up another ventricle… I had known her seventeen days; she'd loved Will for over ten years. Proportion stealthily asserted itself. But why didn't Sue tell him? Why didn't Jess leave Will? Or Will leave Jess? Or threaten Pavel? They were all petrified, unwilling.

And what was I doing? I was a stooge. I felt like I had sometimes in the year of the screens, the world impacting upon me and me just having to learn my lines… I pointed the camera at my face. Maggie would get what she wanted. I looked into the convex eye, and I saw myself. I began to speak quickly, to rant, the booze and the resignation and the decisiveness leaping into words, my broken/healed heart passing incontinently up through my mouth. I walked around the garden, talking, jerking the camera around, drunk with drink and ridiculous. I walked into the wheelbarrow, slicing some skin from my shin. I swore. I went on and I went on. I proclaimed to the camera that Sue loved Will. I went further, declaring that I would force Sue to tell him. I was prone to decisions, I was right as the stars.

I stopped the camera and walked around the lake to the barns. I took out the video tape and left it in Maggie's collage box under the easel on which *Three People Who Love Jessica* sat. I walked through the garden and went to bed, feeling I was a reasonable man with a sense of proportion. Feeling also that mother would be proud of me. I slumbered magnanimously in my four-poster bed.

III

I did not wake magnanimously. The sunshine which bounded into the room with labradorial eagerness seemed only to taunt my lack of health. Several negative things were happening inside my body at once. Most were to do with drinking, but the pre-eminent negativity, the one I felt most likely to endure beyond the early afternoon, involved the hazy recollection of the tape, what I had said on the tape. I re-assembled yesterday's clothes and dashed out of the house to Sue's barns. I twirled around in the courtyard, searching for Maggie, for any sign of Maggie. Sue was there, being laptop beneath the marquee. I needed to breach our covert agreement of distance.

"Have you seen Maggie?"

"Have you seen yourself Ben? Been sleeping in the road?"

"Where's Maggie?"

"Gone, thank God, to London. She's got some arts TV show to record."

"Did she take everything with her?"

"Pavel's here."

"No, I mean her stuff. Did she take her stuff?"

"Pavel's here"

"Sue."

"… I don't know Ben. I don't know. Are you all right?"

I looped around the courtyard, examining nooks and surfaces for the tape. I went inside the barn and looked there. I marched into Maggie's room and confronted a bemused, waking Pavel with my demands. He looked at me and lit a cigarette. All Maggie's things were gone from the room. The tape was gone. I called her on her mobile, it was switched off. I called her at her flat and left a gasping, repetitive message. I went out into the courtyard and marched up to Sue.

"I need to speak to you."

"Need?"

"Yes, need."

"Really?"

"Yes, really."

"Now?"

"Tonight. In the pub. We'll leave about nine. Okay? From here."

"Ben I am impressed."

I marched back up to the house. Will was in the kitchen, cricket commentary trickling already from the paint-splattered radio. He turned to me, "Possible collapse Ben."

"Don't feel that bad."

"I mean England, four for twenty three."

I sat down, and as I became still the world increased its own velocity.

"Not looking too clever Ben, tiring walk?"

"... Listen Will. I need the day off. And you have to come to the pub with me tonight."

"But I've..."

"Will I need it."

"… But they always have that TV on in there. "

This was evidently the height of barbarism. But he frowned in a martyr's smug gloom and offered a nod signifying capitulation.

"Good. I'll see you at nine, here. Don't tell Jessica where you're going. Don't be late."

Will perked up a little at the mention of deceiving his wife and smiled, a series of parallel valleys folding into his forehead. He called me "Clandestine Ben" as I walked from the room and hummed the music from *The Thirty-Nine Steps*.

I needed to speak to someone I could trust. I needed the friend without an angle. *Mammy!* This was the reason for the day off. I went into the study and called her. The phone rang tremendously. She was breathless when she answered, "I was out in the garden love. The hedgehog came again last night."

"I need to see you mum."

"You all right? Everything okay?"

"Yes. I need to speak to someone."

She was suspicious and flattered, galvanised into use, "When you coming?"

"Nowish?"

"I'll put the kettle on."

I went upstairs and showered then I shaved and put on my new, light Savile Row suit, the Chardonnay one. I needed all the help I could get.

Mother was in the kitchen, leaning over the table on which was spread a tabloid horoscope, "Reading yours love, powerful alignments."

I did not approach her, so she stood and walked forward. She stopped in front of me and extended her hands, palms cupping the tops of my arms and her fingers lacing round to the back of my shoulders. She patted me four times.

"What a beautiful suit. Can't be one of your father's?"

"I was bought it by a friend, she's..."

"Is that your problem love? A woman?"

"No. Yes. Can I have a cuppa mum?"

She smiled utterly; benignly. She smiled like all sons everywhere want mothers to smile always. She walked slowly to the kettle and tipped steaming water into a mug. Deliberately, it was the mug I favoured as a child. It had a transfer of two curly-haired, good-hearted outlaws across it. They were leaning across the bonnet of a red car whose contours suggested japes and inordinate speed.

I sat down at the table. She took the chair next to mine and angled it out so she was facing me. Did I tell her everything? I hope not. I excluded the contact lens lost in the pubic mound; I excluded certain malign thoughts I'd had about Will; I excluded most of what I had said on the tape. She got the girls and the boys bit – the unrequited love and the lonely hearts and the disappointed lives. That was easy. She got the sections about me being lost and lonely and just not knowing what to do. That was normal. But she didn't get the bit about my accidental artistic career, "But you can't draw love. You got an E in your exam. I remember that. You drew that onion that looked like a boil."

Nor did she seem concerned about the tape.

"Look mum, I told some secrets, secrets that could hurt people. When Maggie sees it she'll be in heaven. She hates them all now. They insulted her, she'll use it to hurt them."

"Some people need hurting sometimes. I'm sorry love but it's true."

She sighed deeply and looked across the kitchen to the tiles fixed behind the sink and the marbled breakfast bar.

Then she turned to me quickly, and in a voice as low and as charged as confessional, she said, "I never liked Will. I know your father loved him. He bought him that white linen suit and pretended it was old so Will wouldn't be embarrassed. But I never liked him. He was bad for you. He made you want more. He made you want more than we could give. You have to remember that they're different. They're not like us Ben, the rich, they're not like us at all. Forget that girl Sue, forget her, you want a nice girl with strong hands, not too pretty, not too clever. Why don't you move back in here? We can manage. I've got the money from your father."

She wept then and I held her. And I felt the swell and switch of the generations, for I was her protector now and she was now my child.

After lunch we left the house and walked the slim road up towards the churchyard. The only traffic was in the sky, a single gleaming plane leaving a falling gas of white behind it in the blue. A rounded pigeon pecked lackadaisically into the pebbles which fronted the village hall. I held her hand. I liked her hair now, had grown used to her widow's tints. I accepted that she must make a life. Her need to give would make her seek someone, and someone's need to take would find her. I hoped that whoever waited in time for her would be good. I hoped we could be friends..? not mates, not drinking buddies, but cordial, warm. Yes, as long as he was warm, and let her be warm to him, I didn't care who he was. I hoped he'd wear braces though. I don't know why, but I hoped that.

We walked beneath the sturdy wooden porch which announced the entrance to the churchyard. We skirted the church, moving passed its drear buttressing, and we came to the back of the yard. A buckled fence of green plastic mesh collapsed in all directions, and beyond it plumed the brown of a fallow field. The soil slowly sloped to a raggy copse of young trees, themselves cluttered with cruddy, broken farm machines. The field was empty. Where were all the farmers these days? Indoors I suppose, emailing the government about agriculture policy.

We stopped at a grave and looked down. My father's name, then his birth and death years – a single hyphen between. Life as hyphen. Three words were written below the dates, carved then painted into dark grey stone: *A Good Man*. My mother chose that. I couldn't have done any better. The grey stone was improbably smooth, like liquid. *A Good Man* – what else to say?

❧

I returned to Will's house in the late afternoon and went straight to my room. I prowled from window to window, from bed to suit of armour, from door to wall, then I fell onto the bed and set my alarm for 8:30. I tried to sleep. For a long time I could not and I studied the changing arc of the sun, my neck enfolded by the huge pillow, my ears tickled by it.

I fell into a reverie. On the cusp of sleep I began to think that people were cars. They drove along roads which bristled with enigmatic suns and markings, cracking into each other and blaming each other. All the brittle, armoured people, shouting at others for being reckless, while themselves being reckless. One of the cars was Sue, she drove quickly with apparent conviction, her bodywork gleaming and beautiful, but inside the sound of the engine banged and chugged and her boot was ripe with rotting contraband. And Jessica was a sports car, a nippy red cliché of a motor; empty, except for an overnight bag filled with cosmetics and cocaine and a single pair of black knickers. She pelted down chaotic highways, forcing other drivers from the road. Will was there too, a charming sedate old motor, a vintage Anglophile's ride, rammed into a verge, stalled, radio twittering away to the sky – waiting in smiling rage for someone to fix him.

The alarm woke me and I showered and went downstairs. Will and Jessica were in the kitchen, Jess with magazines, Will with *Wisden*. Archie sat on the table, his legs stretched out in front of him. He was banging a plastic figure into the tabletop. Jess "Shushed" him and returned to her reading. Will looked up and eyed me conspiratorially, he nodded and gently pushed the chair out behind him. Jessica glanced upwards, sensing his awkwardness. Her eyes were a question.

"Going to the pub with Ben."

She smiled, "On the tiles boys?"

"Something like that."

"Good, good."

I imagined Pavel, Pavel's body entering her mind.

Will leaned over and kissed Archie on the forehead, "Keep an eye on him."

"Yes Will, and I won't forget..."

"I'm just saying..."

"Come on Will," I intervened.

"Have a good night boys. And if you bring the barmaid back to share, don't wake me. Unless you want me to take some *piccies*."

Will lifted his jacket from the coat peg and walked from the kitchen, heading towards the front door. I motioned towards the back, "This way."

"It's quicker," he said, indicating the counter direction.

"We've got to get Sue."

Will looked puzzled, but did not ask questions.

We walked down through the garden and round the lake. Sue was not outside, so we walked to the largest barn. Pavel was in the kitchen, talking on Sue's portable phone. I guessed it was Jess on the line and that she had called him as soon as we had left the house. Pavel froze as we passed. In the corridor I heard him hang up. We went upstairs.

Sue was at one of the two computers at the far end of the room. She was typing while talking into a small microphone which dangled across her mouth, connecting to her phone. She turned around to face us and held up her hand. She mouthed, "Five minutes."

I wondered what was meant by "Five minutes". In my experience it could mean any amount of time. We sat down on the sofa midway down the room. Will tried to cajole me into revealing what I was up to, but I bobbed my head around non-committally and he seemed content to wait. I looked upwards to the acres of skylight which roofed the barn. The trees were utterly still, the light still strong.

After five minutes she stood and walked over.

"Ready Sue?"

"For what?"

I ignored her question.

The three of us walked downstairs. Pavel had disappeared from the kitchen. I was ahead and walked outside, stepping on the path that led down to the road.

"We're not walking are we?" Asked Sue.

I stopped and turned, "I thought we would."

"I've got to get back to make some calls."

"Sue," an amused Will implored, "it's only a ten minute walk."

"And ten minutes back. And you stopping to point out a bird or a badger track."

Will laughed, "Okay, I'll get the car. See you out on the road."

He turned and walked back towards his house.

Sue and I moved down the path, branches wagging out across it and the summer light showing the leaves to be crepuscular skin. I could feel Sue walk behind me, her steps reluctant and slow. She stopped.

"Look Ben."

I turned around and looked at her. She was flushed and scared and seemed so small.

"What are you doing?"

My silence was enough to tell her.

She shook her head and looked at the ground, her dark hair falling downwards. She shuffled her feet. I could feel the calculations, the premonitions of loss and gain, of loss or gain, clicking through her mind. For a few moments she almost spoke. Then she raised her head and stared at me. I had never seen fear in her eyes before. I had seen ambition, and that night in Brussels I had seen pity and love I suppose, yes I had seen love in her eyes then. But never this. It was the terror of powerlessness. And I know that to call Sue powerless seems wrong – her life is an aphrodisiac of control and money – but that was what it was. She wanted to break things, rip things up, I could see that in her eyes, the vandal fever of entrapment.

She seemed so lost and stupid to me then. Her nails clicking against each other and those white and small pumps, flapped out at absentminded angles. It occurred to me that if Will did not know, then he could never actually refuse Sue. And Sue could continue to dream: no exposure, no rejection – inviolable hope. And Sue's dream, I felt sure at that moment, Sue's dream of Will was what kept her going, what kept her working, and earning and cutting deals. Because if she had this sense of incompletion, this permanent sense that she had never been satisfied, then her hunger would remain; thrive and sharpen. The hunger would froth and gnash and declare and demand precious and rarefied substitutes.

But what did I know? Was I doing the right thing? Right and wrong! Hear those words! At that moment I could barely spell them. It didn't matter now. This wasn't right and this wasn't wrong. Nothing so cosy, because this was people and this was life. If I didn't tell Will, then I guessed that Maggie would. And what do I get? Who do I get?

And then Sue smiled. It was a dreadful smile and it chilled me, it was meek. And she stepped towards me and pushed her arm around my back, her head onto my shoulder.

"You're right," she said quietly. "You're right, I have to."

She was like my child now, unwilling progeny and

creation. And me? Frankensteinian narrator. She spoke again, suddenly, "What if I can't? I can't. I can't."

But she kept walking forward.

At the end of the path where it met the road, Will was waiting in his car. Sue climbed in the back and I got in the front next to him. The radio was on. Two chubby-sounding men were criticising other men who had played professional sport earlier in the day. We made the pub in two minutes.

When we entered, the landlord was propping his head up with his palm, elbow resting on the dark wooden bar. He was staring at the TV which mumbled in the corner. The news was on – speedy anatomy of world misfortune. I stepped up to buy drinks and Will stepped in front of me, "I'll get these Ben, gardeners can't afford rounds."

"Will sit down," I barked. "You've got no bloody money."

Perhaps I was surprised by this outburst even more than Will. He walked away and the barman looked at me with distaste. I held eye contact with the him to ensure compliance and service, "Three large scotches."

He poured and I turned to see Will and Sue sat quietly at a long table at the far end of the bar.

I sat down and looked at Will. He was wounded.

"Will, I'm sorry. But you can't go on behaving like lord of the manor. You have to wake up."

"Yes, I know, but there's no need to be so bloody rude. I don't want the world to know."

"I am sorry."

I spread the drinks across the table. We looked at each other for a while and Will and I gulped our whiskeys. Sue did not touch hers. I fetched two more and Will and I gulped those, wanting the distraction of objects. Will looked flushed already, he had never been able to take his drink. I stared at Sue, indicating with my eyes that she should speak. She went to the bar.

Will grew agitated and turned to me, "Ben, this is a bit odd. What is going on?"

"She'll tell you," I nodded towards Sue who was returning to the table with more drinks. She sat down.

"What is this Sue? Ben says you have something to tell me."

Sue said nothing for a while, then slowly, "Yes Will, Ben and I are lovers."

Will looked relieved and chipper, he jostled us with buffoonish congratulations, "Excellent, Jess was right."

"Sue, tell Will about the barns. Tell him why you bought them."

Silence.

I tried again, "Sue, tell Will why you commissioned the painting."

Silence.

"Will, Sue has something to tell you about the way she feels."

Again that look, the naked cages of her eyes, bursting nearly. She regained some of her self-possession, "Yes Will, Ben and I agreed that if we ever get married, we'd like you to be the best man."

Will saluted us with bemused positivity, "Excellent, thank you. But why all this cloak and dagger stuff?"

"Will," I decided to take control, "ever since she met you..."

A new music had clattered from the bar TV and Sue, with anger in her voice, said,

"This is the show that Maggie's on." She shouted across to the landlord, "Turn it up," and turned her chair away from the table to face the TV.

Will did the same. He smiled at me. "We'll talk afterwards. I want to see this."

So the three of us sat in the pub and watched TV.

❧

Intro music completes. Titles cut to studio. Two steps lead to a brown pedestal. Two chairs on the pedestal. Two people on the chairs: A plump woman with large hair and grey complexion; and a thin man with crew cut and diamond earring.

Hi. I'm Dave Diamond. On tonight's Arts Live *special, we'll be showcasing the work of resurgent rock idol Danni Red, formerly of platinum-selling rock band Mudfugger. Though currently facing charges of petty theft, the on-bail rocker will perform two live tracks for us, taken from his planned comeback album,* Shagging Mates' Wives. *But first, an interview with the ubiquitous and terrible infant of British art, Maggie Twist who'll be reviewing the latest work from a promising young artist, then talking about her own 'work in progress'. Good evening Maggie.*

Davey.

Er. Before we come to your work, we're going to take a look at a mysterious young artist who also works as a gardener. We've been

hearing a lot about him recently and you've been closely associated with his development. Can you tell us a bit about him?

I met him at a party and recognised his talent immediately. He's been filming for me since then and I've been teaching him a few things. And this morning I took possession of a new tape, his first truly solo work.

It's been said that this gardener is the first artist of a new school. What do you make of that Maggie?

I agree. His work does transcend existing concepts of art. It captures the chances and mistakes on which entire lives turn. He is a maestro of the accident. But his work is never flashy, never draws attention to itself, it is modest work. It makes you ask, "Did he even mean to do this?" This is the zenith of his professionalism. He makes you think, "I could do this." But of course you can't. Just try and make a film like this one and you'll realise what I mean. The simulated drunkenness in this piece is brilliant.

So tell us about the film Maggie.

Like all his work, it doesn't have a title. I'm calling it the *Garden Tape*. It was filmed solo and at night in one of the gardens which he tends, and it's a very, very, personal piece, certainly his most personal to date.

Here we go then. Ben the Gardener's latest film, fêted as the crystallising work in the 'Accidents and Modesty' movement.

IV

Will turned to Sue, "Is it true?"

"Yes."

"And the barns and the painting?... Why didn't you?"

"Jess, I..."

"Jess. Jessica is. We might..."

"Shut up Will."

"It's true, we might of..."

"Shut up Will. Please shut up."

Will ordered more drinks.

Sue called me a "prick".

I bought a bottle over the bar.

The landlord threw us out.

Could it be raining now? It seemed to be. As we entered the pub, the sky was as clear as a monk's complexion – now it was dark with cloud and rain. Will sloshed into the driver's seat. It took me several attempts to locate the appropriate piece of car to open. Sue hung back then tapped on the driver's window. Will wound it down.

"You shouldn't drive Will."

"Should."

"Will, you shouldn't drive."

"Should. Can. Bloody will. Village tradition, drunk drunk driving."

Still Sue baulked, "Will?"

Decisively, "Piss. Off."

Sue soberly climbed into the front passenger seat.

I sat in the back, in the centre of the seat, one hand on each of the seats in front of me, steadying my drunken, lolling head. Sue put her feet up on the car seat and pulled her knees up beneath her chin, sliding her palms beneath her pumps. She stared at the windscreen. I stared at the windscreen. Will lunged beneath the wheel. His keys scratched against the black plastic of the steering column, "It's gone. They've stolen the ignition."

Sue leaned over and took the keys from his hand, sliding them into place.

The car chomped forward and out onto the road. Sue leaned over and flicked on the wipers. Two arcs of clarity formed across the wet glass. Will changed gears, incorrectly, then changed gears again. Nobody spoke. Rain pattered onto the car.

What had I done? It was difficult to tell. I would leave it until the morning to think about it. Or perhaps the afternoon, the next day, week. Maybe I would never think about it, ever. What had I done?

We moved through the village: house, mother; graveyard, father; church, empty. The village was grey now and the wet trees were grey green and the road was grey also, black grey. Will leaned forward and studied the road, his nose almost against the glass, his chin touching the wheel. Sue looked out of the side window, her head turned away from me. My hand was close to her shoulder, gripping the back of her seat. We were almost touching. Water sluiced into the gutters of the road. The sky was weeping, maudlin drunk.

Will stopped the car at the right hand turn that led into his copious drive. There were no other cars, but he ceremoniously flicked up his indicators and checked all his mirrors, studiously overcompensating for his lack of co-ordination. The car stood still in the rainy road and the indicator clicked infuriatingly.

"Will, there are no other cars."

"Safety Sue, I'm checking."

"Will there are no other cars."

"Checking Sue."

Will bobbed his vision quickly again between mirrors and turned the wheel slowly to the right. The car stalled across the road and Will fumbled and swore; he fumbled his swearing and swore at his fumbling and then started the car. I stared at the back of his head, the boyish wisps of hair growing down from the base of his skull, growing down in two lines, like hairy, pointed teeth. I inclined my head and looked at the thick, straight darkness of Sue's hair, speckled with wet from the dash to the car. We broached the drive and bumbled along its pebbly arc, up towards the house, rocking through potholes and under trees. Wet horses stared at us from beneath a leaking canopy. I imagined their smell. We made the top of the drive and rattled into the courtyard.

Knowing he had beaten Sue in the matter of his drunk drunk driving; knowing also that he was confused and distressed and ever-so-slightly mad, Will pressed down onto the wet black accelerator. The car lurched forward, picking up speed, gravel lifting up from the tyres as Will swung the car round to berth in habitual space…

Then I saw Archie through the rain-plashed screen, a little ghost standing in pyjamas before us on the gravel. Will saw him too, saw Archie staring at the long, wet-silvered bonnet, as it sleeked towards him; and looking along it also, looking up to see his drunken father behind the liquorice steering wheel.

Archie's eyes were wide, his body hung and static. Will shouted and twisted furiously and the car forced beyond the boy, missing him. He twisted again and with sharp, metallic dullness we cracked into stone or wood, or something. Then the car was sound and a whiteness tossed upwards – a face disappearing past silvery auto glass. Then bones, jumbling in their bag across the roof. We turned and through the back window saw a white shape slump down onto the gravel.

Will jumped from the car and ran and lifted Archie, holding him tightly as the boy began to cry. He released him slightly, looking into the boy's face and pushing his wet, plastered hair up and off his forehead.

"Archie. We nearly killed you. Archie, Archie, what are you doing?" Will said in fever.

"'Scapin'."

"God boy. God."

I climbed out. Sue was already at the back of the car, standing over a body, her eyes wide as Archie's, her body shaking already. I crouched down and turned the body. Pavel. A streak of blood running from his temple and diluted already by the rain. I put my finger to his neck to feel for a pulse. I had never done that before. I tried the wrist, nothing. An ear to his heart. I heard the engine humming behind me, and I heard Archie's tears. The blood still came through. Did that mean his heart was moving? I listened again... it wasn't. But the blood?... Such a small cut. But on the temple, the weak and prominent place. Why is it called that? Doctors call me, doctors fax me.

"Get a fucking doctor. Get a fucking ambulance." That was me.

Sue just stood there. Her mouth silent and her body saying, 'Why? Why get a doctor? He's a dead man.'

Pavel looked so beautiful in the rain, his white T-shirt mimicking his cooling shape and the tint of his dark, wet skin pushing through the white also. And that trickle of blood, its redness so red for a moment then diluted by the rain and the rain. He looked so beautiful, like an advert for crashing. I had always liked Pavel's hair, always wanted mine to be like it. He was so beautiful and so dead and so wet and so beautiful and dead.

And Sue just stared at me, and stared at Pavel, then stared back at me until, I guessed, she couldn't tell who was dead and who was alive. I knew though, I knew. Ask me, test me, I know. Then Sue climbed back into the car, into the driver's seat, and she held the wheel and ran her fingerprints across it. She slid the driver's seat forward, to fit her legs, then she grabbed the wheel and pushed back against the head-rest, rubbing the back of her head into it, strands of her hair sticking. She put her wet shoes on the pedals and she pushed them violently. And I thought Sue, Sue, that's not going to help.

Will began to stride towards the house, his steps wiry with anger. Before he got to the doorway, he was shouting for Jessica, his voice taut and hoarse already, cracking beyond its registers. Jessica was about to hear an escalated version of Will's 'Neglect' speech.

Then Sue shouted, "Will. Come here."

He turned to acknowledge her and to acknowledge that he wasn't going to stop.

"Will." The voice was strong now – tones of edict or commandment: Biblical, totalitarian voice.

Will stopped and held eye contact with Sue long enough to obey. He turned around. Sue reached out and took my hand and pulled me towards her. Her face was wet and red and cold, like Autumn. Was it wrong of me to find her beautiful then? Or wrong to see the bloody peace of Pavel's face as somehow right? Let me be wrong then. Will stopped and looked down at the sodden body. I have never seen an expression like the one on his face at that moment. Pity was there. And relief – a wide sneer of relief – and terror was there also. It was not truly an expression, it was compression – a compression of feelings which normally do not touch – are not felt to touch – but which chance and accident and death unify into the muscles of a face. It was a look that I will never forget, hope never to see again.

Sue took Will's hand also and moved him near us. Archie was clamped onto his father's torso, shivering. Will scraped his lips through the parting of hair that ran from Archie's soft crown. We stood there in the rain, a huddle of shock – the unprecedented making us refugees. Sue looked at Will,

"I was driving."

Will's eyes seemed huge and they seemed to bounce.

She continued, "I'm sober. I have no motive. There will be publicity but no charges."

"No Sue, no, no. It was an accident."

"I'm not sure it was."

"But he was just there."

"So was Archie."

"Sue, no. No."

"Will, you have killed your wife's lover. I was driving."

He shook his head.

"Then go to prison. What will it do to your boy?"

Will grew quiet and defeated.

Sue turned to me, "Ben?"

It was so cold.

"Sue was driving."

❧

We walked inside. I wiped my feet on the doormat as I entered. Sue kept Will close to her. Each time I blinked I saw an image of Pavel laying on the wet, pebbled courtyard. In the kitchen, two half-filled gatherings of paradoxically-travelling particles imitated glasses. A ruby trickle curled from the base of a green bottle. It was Will's favourite claret. The radio emitted orchestral music which I knew but could not place. We went into the lounge.

Jessica was curled on a sofa, Pavel's jumper placed over her torso, a sleeve touching the carpet. Her long, thin skirt was bunched up, high on her long, smooth legs. The room smelled of sex, of his and hers. She was dozing, but she roused slightly at the footsteps in the room.

"Did you find Archie, Pavel? Where did he get to?"

She roused further, opened her eyes and inclined her face towards us. She sat up quickly, and brushed her skirt over her legs. I had never seen Jessica flustered before. She stared at Will, at Sue, at me. We dripped onto the rug. Nobody spoke. Then Sue told Jess about Pavel, told Jessica how she had just killed him. Jessica thought she was asleep, hoped she was asleep. Then she knew she wasn't, but still hoped, somehow, that she was. She blinked and blinked. Then she snarled "Liars" and ran from the room.

The au pair padded into the room, meek and confused. Sue sent her away with a glance. Sue caught my eye and nodded towards the drinks cabinet. She held up three fingers. I opened an aged and ostentatious bottle of brandy. I poured three large measures into three glasses, took a gulp, and stepped towards Will. He was stood in the centre of the room, beginning to shiver, looking at nothing with wide open eyes. Archie was still melded against him. Will took a glass from me and offered an ugly, broken smile.

Jessica ran back into the room. She had seen. Sue took the third glass from the top of the cabinet.

"Will you bastard. You weak, jealous little bastard. Is this how you win? Is this how you win me?"

"Jess," Sue spoke very slowly, "Jessica. Listen. I killed Pavel. I killed him."

Jessica stared through Sue for a moment then lunged towards Will. She slid her hand between her husband and her child, and pulled the boy towards her. She crammed Archie against her, kissing his head fervently. She whispered to the child,

"What are we going to do? What are we going to do now?"

Will stared and tilted brandy down his throat. Jessica fell back onto the sofa, Pavel's jumper coiled at her feet, her child held in to her. Sue stepped towards her and handed over the brandy. Jessica gulped, her shaking hands tight around the glass. Sue again motioned to me, and we stepped outside the room into the corridor.

"Make some tea. Lots of sugar. Call the police. Then call Maggie. You up to that?"

I wasn't.

"Yes."

She kissed me on the cheek and I watched her turn and walk back into the lounge. And though I loved her in that moment, I did not want her: not her time or support, not her sex, her money or laughter, nor her love. I simply loved her. I loved the way she loved Will. I had never seen love like it. A love that thinks quickly, and is hard. A clever love. I looked at Sue as she pushed the door open, looked at her small back and her strong, wet black hair and her stubby fingers that clenched and unclenched by her side, and I loved the Sueness of Sue.

This revelation did not last. In the kitchen I put the kettle on. On the radio, two keen people discussed the plight of immigrants in 'Fortress Europe'. I knew a little about that now. There was a repelled invader on the drive. I picked up the radio and cracked it down on the oh-so-rustic tiles. I was relieved and surprised by my actions. I noticed I was crying. I opened my throat and accepted brandy, then I picked up the sleek, black phone and called the police. After that, I called Maggie on her mobile. She picked up immediately.

"Hello?"

"Maggie, it's Ben."

"Did you see the show Ben? You're a star."

"Yes I saw the show."

"That was indiscreet of you, talking about Will and Sue like that. I got your messages but I had to use the tape. Art transcends our private needs."

"Pavel's dead."

She didn't believe it. All the way from London to Suffolk in the black cab, she didn't believe it. She believed it when she saw the body though, fenced around by the gaudy plastic tape which police everywhere prize for its luminous properties. She believed it then. But I'm sure as the days and the weeks went on she mostly forgot it again and expected to see him, to smell him, to feel him. Until one day, probably months on, she really believed it, really knew. And who knows, maybe she quite liked it.

I stood alone in the kitchen for some time and felt numb. I thought of one of Donald's paintings. It was a piece of his from the early, nihilistic days, when he was moody. Donald pronounced that the piece had "Gone beyond abstraction". He said that it "began Substraction, Astraction. Urstraction".

It's like this:

Exactly like that.

V

The next day I walked down to Sue's. It was perversely sunny. I looked around the barns and found her in the bedroom. She was thrusting clothes into a large black suitcase. She said "Oh" when she saw me and continued to pack. The bedroom window was open and the light curtains hung and lifted in the breeze. I looked at her for a while then said, "Okay?"

I tried again, "You leaving?"

She exhaled and turned to face me, "Going to stay in London."

I sat down on the bed and smoothed the rumpled sheet. "Sue, I can't stay at Will's."

"Stay at your mum's."

"I can't, she'd…"

She reached into her suitcase and lifted out a bunch of keys. She threw them towards me. "Stay as long as you want."

"How long will you be away?"

"I don't know. A week? Forever?"

She closed her case and walked towards me. Her lips felt cold on my cheek. I followed her after a while and went out into the courtyard. I saw her walking down the tree-lined path towards the road, her stubby hands clutching her black bag. The horn of an impatient taxi lifted from the road and startled two pigeons, themselves lifting, up from the trees. Bye bye, baby.

I spent the night in her bedroom, in her bed. I could smell her on the pillows. I did not sleep much. I imagined Will and Jess in their tearful dawns, facing finally the actual shapes of their lives. I imagined Archie also, quiet perhaps or roaring with tears, the events of the previous night snagging inside him. And I thought of Maggie. Maggie didn't really matter to me. Pavel didn't matter either, the deplorable truth of the darkness told me. I did think of him though, Pavel and his dead and Archie-coloured skin. When I did sleep I dreamed of my friend Paul. The one I went to school with who held up a juggernaut with a black stick. I dreamed I was in Queensland with him and we carved a mango into the shape of a gun.

Will came to see me three days after the accident. I was sat under the yellow marquee, eating toast. Again, the glaring sun misjudged the mood. Will looked at his shoes. Their brogue patterning was skilfully crafted, but not as absorbing as he simulated. I stared at him throughout. His jaw ground round and round, teeth pushing against each other.

"Thank you for the other night Ben."

"   "

"I mean it. Thanks. I feel..."

"What you going to do now?"

"Travel for a while. We're going to stay with my parents in France, then go to hers in Singapore. They'll look after the boy while Jess and I go off for a bit. Patch things up. The au pair's gone this morning."

"She believes it, doesn't she? Doesn't she Will?"

"How do you mean Ben?"

"Jess believes it was Sue?"

"Yes. And the police."

"Will she forgive her?"

"I don't know."

"Will you tell her later, when the inquest's over?"

"I don't know. I…"

When I was twelve I read First World War books, some about life on the Western Front. When a new soldier arrived in the trenches the veterans could tell if he would live or die in the mud. Some had a glow around them, an aura of luck and the old hands stuck close by. I used to think of Will in this way. Did I still? Yes. Though now I will not stick close to his luck. I'd rather be shot in the mud.

"You can live in my house while we're gone."

"I'll come and get my things."

He looked chastened for a moment, then, "Where's Sue?"

"London."

"If you see her..."

"I will."

"And Ben, you won't..?"

I lifted my finger and put it to my lips. No I won't say anything Will, I won't say a word. But not because of you. No, not because of you. My lips are closed for Sue. I do it to honour Sue.

He walked away, the sunshine dancing round him, and the single plane in the sky scribing in white the 'i' of his name which the sun then dotted. I went inside and put more bread in the toaster. I dropped to my knees and wept.

❧

In the days I spent alone at the barns I wanted nothing. No, not true, there was something very precise that I wanted, and wanted dearly. I wanted to be left alone. Formless time moved through me as I read in the barns and walked through the fields. When I felt safe I went up to Will's house to get my things. The house was shut up, deserted. They'd left for France – love rediscovered and hurts healed?

I lifted the loose brick on the back patio that had sheltered the spare key during my childhood. It was still the place. I let myself into the house and walked around. Motes of dust circled in light that climbed through the gaps between curtains. There was a note in Will's handwriting on the kitchen table. It told me to come and go as I pleased and listed some contact numbers. Jessica had signed it too, her writing was taut and rounded and pristine. Archie had daubed an imperfect circle at its base. I tore the circle from the note and put it in my pocket. They had left a bottle of wine out on the table. I uncorked it and poured, walking aimlessly around the house for a while, drifting in the silence and sadness.

I stood for a long time in Jessica and Will's bedroom. I had no thoughts. I took my things from my former room and walked out, slapping the suit of armour as I did so. I went into the lounge and took all of the video tapes that looked interesting, then I returned to Sue's and finished off the wine.

I lay on the sofa, and when my mind had stilled to dumbness, I resolved to become the village idiot: walking deserted lanes at dawn and twilight; cackling unsettlingly at my own jokes in the pub; talking to myself as I dug up flowers and fertilised weeds – single, poor, flat of cap, inane of grin. It seemed the perfect life. I would stay in the village forever, I thought, resenting the building of new houses, the interlopers who would come in, no doubt, and refurbish the pub. I would develop a guarded friendship with the postman and bike six miles to the supermarket then only buy peas. I would stay in the barns until Sue kicked me out, then live in a shed with a gas ring and kettle in her grounds.

A couple of men turned up at the barns one night. They knocked on the door and when I didn't answer they stalked around the buildings and courtyard. I guessed they were reporters. I got an old broom and leaned out of the top window, pointing the wood at them like a gun. I shouted, "Get off my land." They saw me and ran off. I liked doing that. I laughed to myself for a while and drank a lot of Sue's whiskey. I drank a toast to Paul.

The phone rang twice one day. The first call was from Sue, she didn't stay on the line long, didn't want to talk.

"Ben."

"Sue? Sue, I'm…"

"I've signed the barns over to you. They're yours."

"I? Where are you going to live?"

"Here, London, for a while. I'll be needed at the inquest. Then, who knows? Fuck this island. New York maybe? The Philippines?"

"Sue, the barns, you can't."

"I have. Don't you want them?"

"Of course. But..."

"You earned them as much as anyone Ben."

"Sue, are you okay?"

"I have to go."

"Don't I have to sign..."

But she'd already gone.

The second time the phone rang it was Donald. He wanted to talk and stayed on the line a long time. He'd got the number from my mother. He was coming to England.

Donald came to stay with me in the barns. He intended to stay for a week but he spent over a month with me. He was thinner than when I had seen him last and he wore a preposterous beard. I told him it was stupid and he shaved it off. I decided to feed him up. On the first night, we carried the huge table down from Will's dining room and placed it at the edge of the lake. We got dressed up, me in my Savile Row pinstripe and Donald in Will's wine-stained number. We placed candelabras on the table and sat distantly, one at each end.

Donald had found an old mascara of Sue's and painted an impossibly curling moustache onto his top lip. He shouted "What?" a lot, pretending he couldn't hear me. He occasionally called me an "old dog". He seemed to find that incredibly funny. We feasted on vegetables from the garden, meat from Sue's freezer and claret from Will's cellar. We were hearty and pleased with our eccentricity, pleased to see each other also. We drank a lot that night, then headed off to Will's greenhouses to find weed. Donald recited dialogue from *Casablanca* and *It's A Wonderful Life* as we fell asleep under the trees.

He set up his studio in the barns where Maggie had painted. *Three People Who Love Jessica* was still in there, leaning against a wall. Donald liked it, he said it was "enigmatic, haunting". I told him it was "shit". "Yes," he replied, puffing his words out with his cigarette smoke, "Yes Ben, it's certainly shit. Deliberately shit. That's the difference." I thought that was tosh.

One night we were rolling drunk, reminiscing about our fruit farm days, and I persuaded Donald to film me while I smashed up the painting. I sawed it in half, quarters, eighths, then I jumped up and down on it. I started to cry when I'd finished. Donald hugged me and told me they were all "bastards". I hadn't told Donald the full story then, I still didn't want to talk about it. So it was nice of him to be so supportive. I posted the tape to Maggie, care of her gallery. I wrote *Deliberate Immodesty* on it, as a title for the film. I thought she'd like that but she never got back to me.

I introduced Donald to my mother. He flirted with her and told her he liked the colour of her hair. He called her by her first name. She thought Donald was brilliant, she told him about the onion I'd drawn in my exam that looked like a boil. Donald did a canvas the next day called *Ben's Boil*; it was bright yellow. He gave it to her and she put it up in the lounge. She didn't like it much, but she was happy to have a present.

Sue was on the news one night. She was walking out of the courtroom, holding hands with Dave Diamond. I guess they got back together. She looked beautiful; I was sad and pleased about that. I tried quickly to record the item, but the news had progressed to the business stories before I got the tape in. A verdict of accidental death was recorded. Was that right? I don't know. Accidental life may have been more accurate: for Pavel, for father, for Sue, for us all – also for giraffes and camomile bushes?

I got a bit crazy that night and I told Donald everything. He loved the bit about the contact lens in the pubic hair, he said, "We'll get some old carpet and a glass plate and mock that up tomorrow."

But Donald's special pleasure was saved for the story of my artistic career. If I had to describe his laughter when I told him about my film's TV exposure, I would say that 'Donald whooped and hollered'. He laughed for a long time. I was upset at first, I was serious still, but then I started to laugh as well.

When he had calmed down, I told Donald of the hard and negative feelings I had about Will. He became grave and said "that's sad" a lot, he sucked his teeth, then asked me again how long I'd known Will. I told Donald that I'd slept with Jessica three nights after I returned from Brussels.

Donald invented a new punctuation mark. He said, "You have marks to convey animation and excitement – exclamation marks and italics – but nothing for the down moods. It's *not* fair! We need a punctuation mark that expresses sadness or whimsy. Something for de-emphasis."

He was right. Donald came up with the idea of a downwards pointing triangle.

I was sad when Donald left ▼ He was too, said he was going to live in Bogota. He didn't know why. It was Autumn when he went. I turned the heating on in Will's walled garden. The boiler worked. I fixed that. It was me. Then it was winter. When I closed my eyes, before I went to sleep, I sometimes saw Will and Sue, and sometimes I saw myself also. Nobody wanted it to be cold, nobody chose that. But I loved the frost that gathered on the lake and I loved the naked, twisted trees. There were times when I liked myself and times when I did not. I drank coffee and I wrote this book.

I sold one of the barns to a famous novelist. He was killing himself in the city with drink and drugs. He needed to get out. He didn't mind that the barns weren't finished, he said he liked it. He said he was going to write about the death of the countryside. That seemed a bit silly. I laughed when all those 0s appeared in my bank account. My mum cried when I paid for her to have a conservatory built on the back of her house. It took me a whole day to convince her I wasn't a criminal.

I flew to Bogota to get drunk with Donald. Then we flew out to Easter Island. It was a whim. We went to see the statues. Huge, rude granite heads, facing out to sea. Spooky. On our last day on the island, we stood on the shoulder of a hill, tufts of pale flowered grasses flicking across our boots. We looked beyond the statues, out onto the sea, and we saw the way the light fell onto the breakers. We drank hokum local booze and spoke about the light. It was good to have the salt air on our faces. Donald's satellite phone trilled unanswered in his daybag.

ACKNOWLEDGEMENTS

Light owes a "Howdy" to old, out-of-print science-fiction writer Kilgore Trout.

Thanks to Anna for her support, encouragement and eagle eyes; to Charlie Onians, Susie Jones, Keith Hart, Ciaran Madden, Frans Green, Danny Yank and Cathy Fischgrund for their early input, and to Andrew Chapman and Paul Lenz for their recent editing. Thanks also to Nicholas Royle.

By the way, I did finally wrestle that long, truculent novel out. It's called *Cloven*.

The Group, by Ravinder Chahal

ISBN 1 905315 01 5 • £7.99

"How far can you really take it? I mean, could you lie to someone, get them hooked? Get them believing in something because they want to, for whatever reasons they have of their own, and then come clean? Would they listen to you then or would they just want to keep believing the lie that they've made their own?"

The Group is a book that talks to people who are successful in an economy that they do not believe in. Aimed at those for whom it is fashionable to be knowing, it tells the story of Khaled, an arch-cynic for whom everyone is a fake or a loser. The only problem is Khaled has done very little himself that he can be proud of and is beginning to bore himself.

Faced with the prospect of drifting through life in obscurity he dreams up a satirical scam to reveal how easily people can be manipulated, and how thin their dreams and aspirations are. But rather than escape The Group, his scam only serves to show how hollow he has become, and how he needs to completely recalibrate his own life.

The Group is a dark and wickedly funny book about people who tell lies and people who believe them.

Grief, by Ed Lark

ISBN 1 905315 02 3 • £6.99

"The clouds were ugly and dark as scabs. I loved Keeku for a moment. A cab drove past me and I pretended it was a horse, swore it was a horse. I chased it down the street telling it to giddy-up. I hated Keeku now, the stupidity of her beautiful neck, the docile barges of her thighs and her mouth with the wet hole in it where the words came out."

Juan has left his past behind for the seductions of the city and the Crystal Realm - a world of ever-changing fashion, daily plastic surgery, mind-altering drugs and bizarre sex.

He effortlessly climbs the social hierarchy, gaining money and power until the city thrills to his every move - but something is missing from his life, which perhaps only the picaresque troupe of troubadours who are trekking across the desert in search of him can explain.

Grief is both a unique dystopia, or perhaps an interpretation of the present, and a remarkable psychological fantasy, disturbing, witty and moving by turns.

aboutreverb

reverb isn't a traditional publisher. We think of it as a cross between an online community of readers and an independent record label. Why a record label? Because we publish books that have broadly the same 'sound' - contemporary literary fiction with an edge. This edge can be humorous, it can be thought-provoking, but it is something that makes the book stand out from the crowd. We hope that if a reader has enjoyed one **reverb** book then they will enjoy the others.

reverbforwriters

Unless they are already successful, writers tend to get treated pretty badly. At **reverb** we are trying to do things a little differently:

- **Give new writers a chance -** we are committed to publishing 50 new writers over the next five years.
- **Fast but meaningful feedback -** most traditional publishers will leave unsolicited manuscripts on the slush pile for months; many are rejected unread. At **reverb** we promise to give an answer to any writer who follows our submission guidelines *within seven days*. If we do reject the material we will always try and give a constructive critique rather than simply a three-line rejection letter.
- **Working in partnership -** we view writers as talent to be nurtured rather than a commodity to be exploited. We pay high royalty rates and the lion's share of rights sales always goes to the writer.
- **Developing new talent -** we have dedicated a section of the **readreverb.com** site to information and support for new writers. We will also run free workshops in which our writers will share their experience and knowledge to help new authors develop their work.

aboutreverb

reverbforreaders

Without readers there would be no publishing, so we have set up **reverb**review to create interest in all writers, not just the ones that we publish. **reverb**review is a weekly newsletter that contains book reviews, an in-depth look at an iconic author or book and articles from readers on books that have changed their lives. **readreverb.com** contains an archive of **reverb**reviews, features and news stories from the world of books.

reverbforretailers

Independent booksellers are the backbone of the trade, but more often than not get treated like the poor cousin by large publishing companies. At Reverb we are dedicated to supporting the independent trade through offers, marketing material and author visits.

Printed in the United Kingdom
by Lightning Source UK Ltd.
104846UKS00001B/94-123